DARKENED HORIZONS

ISSUE 3

ISBN 978-1-4357-4999-3

Cover and interior art designed by Gabrielle S. Faust.

TABLE OF CONTENTS

SHALLOW CRIES *Charlotte Emma Gledson*

(5)

ANNUAL CAMPING TRIP *Lloyd Schwieger*

(15)

NATURAL DRIVE *Charles Spencer*

(19)

MIND TRAPPED *Nicole Rogers*

(25)

THE WATCHER AT THE GATE *Alex Rivera*

(43)

APARTMENT J *Gabrielle S. Faust*

(51)

A WALK IN THE SUN *Jim Shifflett*

(65)

THE RED CLOUD AFFLICTION *Stanley Anderson*

(75)

JUST A GIRL *Andrea Colleen*

(95)

THE SLIDING *Kevin Lucia*

(105)

MR. FUCKING BOTHERSOME *Dave Rex*

(117)

NOT A CHANCE *Jessica Lynne Gardner*

(129)

ROUGH NIGHT FOR GLADYS *Colin M. Maguire*

(147)

FLOWER IN THE WIND Rick McQuiston

(167)

DAMNATION OBSERVES *Nickolaus A. Pacione*

(179)

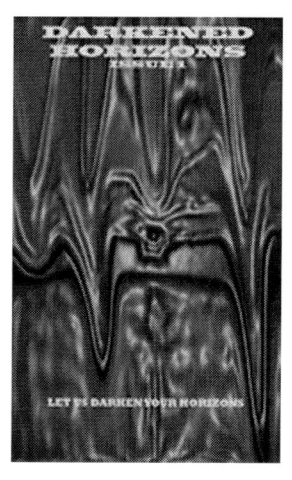

SHALLOW CRIES
By
Charlotte Emma Gledson

Cold winter rain sharply lashed at the window. The wind lulled temporarily.

Sam's laughter reverberated through the room as he pushed the remote control rigidly in the hope his car would gain more speed.

The room was a blush of soft light, flames flickered and danced from the hearth, smoke and fire marrying in unison. A perfect chorus of snaps and crackling firewood filled the air, the pungent earthy scent of wood and charcoal hung in the atmosphere, circulating liberally.

The logs splintered and hissed as Tony sat with his back to the warmth and security of the radiant heat. With a hint of competitiveness, he enthusiastically challenged his son. The cars buzzed and whizzed around the track frantically.

Framed smiling faces that adorned the mantelpiece glowed with beguiling vivacity. The steady tick from the antique Westminster mantle clock was starkly interrupted by somber but lyrical chords that subtly dispersed throughout the room.

"Bath time Sam." Tony uttered to his son as he drained the remaining residue of his Irish malt. He noticed his distorted looks through the arc of color in the crystal glass. He flicked a stray lock of hair that had carelessly fallen across his lined but handsome face.

His dark chestnut hair now contained fragments of grey that enhanced and framed his angular face.

"No, dad!" Sam moaned challengingly. He lowered his head in a sulk, but obediently reached out for the box, and began packing the tracks and cars away. His hair curled around his green eyes, his honey highlights shimmering in the luminosity of the room.

Sam was a smart nine year old. At an age of self awareness he often was temperamental and capricious but Tony enjoyed their intimate times together. Nothing could come between them.

Mari sat silently by a table where a glass bowl of pot-pourri emanated a gentle bouquet.

She remained still as she felt an unyielding love for the child she was watching. She savored the vision that was before her, an overwhelming desire and longing, folded from within, united with the true horror of the knowledge that she would never hold Sam again.

Though she was no longer a physical being, she accepted this ethereal existent. She was able to watch her son in all avenues of his life.

The craving and regret of the absence of physical contact plagued Mari to a degree of obsession. She'd often gaze at her sleeping son and would hum a melody for him if he awoke suddenly, which he often did, overcoming the final threads of a nightmare. She longed to bury her nose in his neck and nestle into him, to feel his breath upon her face. She missed his spontaneous need for her. However, she cherished what she saw, she could see him, and that was a blessing, however small. Sam was too old to yearn for her now, a mere distant thought of a time gone by, but she still implored his love; the pain inside her besieging her constantly.

Sam finally placed the lid on the tatty box. He got to his feet, and went into the alcove of the kitchen which was adjacent to the living room, and joined his father who was pouring himself yet another drink.

"You coming up Dad?" enquired Sam.

"You stay here and load these plates in the washer and I will run your bath OK?"

Tony took a decadent gulp of his drink, refilled his glass, he turned to leave the kitchen.

"Ok Dad, see you up there".

Tony ran up the stairs, two at a time. The spacious Victorian rooms were not consistent with the narrow stairway and halls. His pace reduced as he got to the top of the stairs. He faced the looming hall, where the bathroom awaited him. He hated this hall, its slim corridor ominous in the dim artificial light. But it wasn't the oppressive gloom that left him so unsettled.

As he purposefully strode down the corridor a sudden excruciating memory resurfaced. The pinnacle of the haunting recollection intensified as he entered the bathroom.

Tony searched for the plastic crocodile that twisted around the light cord of the bathroom. It bounced onto his elbow as he blindly swiped the air. The string had been lengthened for Sam in the hope that he would eventually venture into the bathroom alone at night, but he still, to this day found it an insufferable experience. At bath times he insisted that his father sat on the large wicker chair at the back of the blue tiled bathroom, so he would not feel isolated, Tony did this dutifully but with reluctance. He pulled the cord, stark vivid light sparked a raw remembrance of the night that altered his life forever, leaving this room as a dark iconic cloud that would fester in his mind, always.

Mari watched as Sam attentively loaded the dishwasher. She beseeched her son to be able to see her, acknowledge her. She was desperate to hold him and inhale the aroma of his scalp but her arms held no substance. Her feelings were so intense that it almost made her feel complete; complete with heart; with breath; with totality.

Circling around Sam she grabbed desperately but fruitlessly to touch his skin, his soft downy hair, his body. A faint eddy of wind alerted Sam, he looked around to see if a window was ajar; all were closed. He finished loading the final plate, double checked the room in case he had left an item unaccounted for. Feeling chilled, he swiftly finished his job, by getting the soap powder, and sprinkling the granules into the machine.

Mari's feeling of powerless solitude consumed her. She took a step back reluctantly, her arms dropped limply by her side. The dark memory came to the forefront of her mind. A recollection so disquieting she chose to banish it immediately. She turned from her son grudgingly as she turned into the hall. Ascending the stairs she heard the familiar sounds that were coming from the bathroom, her feelings dipping into a pit of heavy-heartedness.

"Dad, done it, I'm coming, just getting something!" Sam yelled loudly up to his father as he bounded up the stairs. But his voice was now drowned by the running water, which gushed loudly and splurged from the ageing taps.

Tony knelt down as he poured the bubble bath into the running water, but in spite of the warm vapor that was forming around him, he felt bitterly cold. Rubbing the back of his neck, it tingled with a sudden chill. Glancing over to the mirror he noticed that it was starting to fog with condensation. He could feel an unnerving aura surrounding him. This familiar yet terrifying presence once again lingered with Tony as he pushed himself up, he rapidly left the bathroom.

Behind the door Mari watched him depart. She began to lift her arms to grab him, but dropped them suddenly and lowered her head.

She took a pace out of the door and her eyes followed Tony as he met Sam coming along the murky hall.

"Going to get ready dad, I will get my water pistol, we can have a fight!" Sam stated enthusiastically.

Tony agreed as he wandered into his bedroom. Here he turned on his bedside radio; the muted sounds of conversation had a welcoming affect on him. He sat on the king-size bed as he often did, and looked at the empty space that lay vacant next to him. The whiskey now taking a negative effect intensified his senses, and also his brooding memories.

Mari, hovering in the hallway watched Sam as he retrieved his pistol and left his room. He hesitated as he loitered in the doorway of the bathroom, and turned back to call for his father.

"Dad, come on!"

As he was finishing his sentence, Tony was coming out from his room.

"Come on, get in will you" Tony's voice held some slight irritation as he marched Sam into the middle of the bathroom.

"I can't baby-sit you every time you have a bath Sam; you are getting too old for this." Tony slumped into the large chair, feeling his body sink into the wicker fibers.

Sam now naked, turned off both taps, and placed his foot cautiously into the water.

"Ok Dad. When I'm ten, I should be fine then shouldn't I?"

Tony smirked, and sipped his drink, the alcohol now warming him, but not eradicating his anxiety totally.

The phone rang; its shrill cry broke the sound of the rippling undulating water that came from around Sam's body as he lowered himself into the bath.

"Well you can start by practicing now, as I answer that bloody phone." Levering himself out of the chair Tony moved clumsily to the door.

Sam protested noisily, splashing with frustration and annoyance as his father departed.

Mari stood opposite the bath, watching Sam as he began to panic due to his father's absence.

It was this moment, as she watched Sam in his vulnerable isolation she re-lived the fateful day, six years ago.

When Mari had delivered her twin sons prematurely after thirty weeks gestation; Jamie's lungs were under developed, causing major problems at the start of his precious life. He soldiered on, defying the doubts of the doctors. Sam's heart had been littered with holes. He endured open heart surgery when he was twelve months old, but being a strong willful individual, he survived the grueling ordeal. The stress and incomprehensible agony traumatized both parents. They lived, breathed, existed, only in the knowledge that the children had to survive. The boys had battled all of their afflictions with great strength, though there were times when things were very strained. Mari and Tony were so vigilant about the state of their health and wellbeing; it caused friction and often opened a rift between them.

When the twins had reached three years old, things had settled down, the compulsion to watch every move lessened, but only slightly.

The twin boys had been happily bathing. Jamie caught Sam innocently on the eye with his toy boat. The sharp plastic pierced Sam's delicate, pale skin, blood surfacing from the laceration. Blood dribbled down Sam's body, marbling his pale skin with crimson streaks. Swiftly Mari had wrapped him up in a towel and carried him to her bedroom to find the first aid box.

Alone, Jamie he began to cough, gently at first, and then began to gasp desperately. An excruciating pain formed within his chest, crushing him as he tried to breathe. The asthma attack left him *choking, gulping for air. His cries useless, the gushing tap drowning out his pleas. When Mari returned, his small lifeless body floated face down, thudding softly and rhythmically against the side of the bath, the water still holding the evidence of his desperate struggles.*

Days later, Mari lay in her own tepid bath water. She closed her eyes as her mind swam with the constant guilt that engulfed her. Appearing suddenly, her husband stormed into the bathroom, hovering above her with an expression that was so startling, his eyes held no clue of what was to come. She attempted to sit up.

Grabbing her hair with sudden violence, he abruptly smashed her head repeatedly against the unforgiving porcelain surface, her skull yielding with every impact. Intense agony shot through every nerve, blood circled and swirled within the perfumed soap suds and bath water, her struggles were useless.

"Murderer", he shrieked maniacally. His wretched face a mask of rage as he held her head beneath the fragrant water. Her last memory of her husband was the utter hatred behind his manic eyes, a glare of insanity that penetrated her being as he continued to demolish her head.

Her life ebbed away like dispersing steam; no heavenly light welcomed her; only a single disturbing, guilty truth. It was her cataclysmic error that cost her, her life, and that of her son, Jamie.

Tony was found guilty for the horrendous crime he had committee and received two years for manslaughter with mitigating circumstances taken into consideration. He had freely and openly admitted his guilt.

Sam's grandmother had nurtured him in those testing years, here in this very house. Tony had written daily to his treasured son as he sat within those confining walls. He patiently waited for the time he would be part of his Sam's life once more. Eventually as a free man, he returned to the family home that harbored his ugly deed.

Here Mari was caught in the perpetual state of purgatory. Protectively, she watched over her son, it was the least she could do but the most she could hope for. Mari's choice was to remain here for her growing child. Her guilt so paramount, she was content to exist in this oblivion.

Sam now sat alone. A dripping tap his only companion. He strained to hear his fathers muffled voice from downstairs.

Mari gazed at Sam intently, imploringly; hating to see her only surviving son alone in the water. Like her son Jamie, Sam had problems at birth.

Mari walked to the side of bath; the compulsive wish for her son to be safe and secure consumed her. She desperately insisted to Sam that he would be fine, daddy would be back to play a water fight, once he was off the phone.

Sam was about to call for his father when a sudden grey pallor shadowed his face. The vision of his putrefying decaying mother, staggering towards him, eyes absent of life, hollow vacant abysses of blackness, was too much for the child.

His heart failing with shock he desperately reached out his slender arm, helplessly seeking assistance, but no strong arms reached down to pull him away from his impending death. No supple bosom of security awaited, to protect him from undeniable doom only an unknown terrifying horror. Sam's agonized screams, calling out his brother's name becoming imperceptible, as he uttered his last strangled plea. His once zestful but nimble being, now devoid of life, sank to the bottom of the deep foamy bath like a heavy leaden weight, his hair haloed around him as the water embraced his fragile corpse.

Beholding the vision before her, yet another death for which she felt wholly responsible, Mari descended into her final torturous hell. Her son ascended into an eternal peace that she so yearned for.

Trapped in the most personal hell of hells, she could only reflect on this pivotal moment for eternity, knowing that everything she had loved so deeply so desperately, was lost forever.

Her silent screams echoed and absorbed the fabric of the building, leaving a penetrating pulse of horror and grief, marooned in the foundations of this once, happy family home.

ANNUAL CAMPING TRIP
By
Lloyd Schwieger

Satan is my heartbeat

Murder is my bone

The bone I have to pick with you

Really turns my crank

Distills all my anger and makes it boil, ping and bark

Bark and howl like the slavering tri-fold jaws of Cerberus

On that blackened day he was manacled

Chained, snarling and snapping, to that unholy, but oh so welcoming

gate

Rage is the fuel that sends me into the berserk of blood that wreathes

the sky

The blood that erupts like wildfire from your screeching, shivering

form

A bone to pick

A bone handled ice pick

Delightfully plunged

Again, as I laugh

Again, as you cry

Again, as I cackle

Again, as you die

Again, into the quivering mass that used to beg and implore

Again, into the broken toothed gash that shall beg and plead no more

The unclean maggots squirming in the accursed dirt of your reeking grave

Sing my name in the shambling tongues of death

The demons of my unfettered hatred are driven to frenzied abandon

By this gruesome song of infernal lust and divine corpulence

They shriek with Hellish force to the heights

Empty eyes now blazing

Mindless minds now bent on rending

The defiled angels fall, wailing, to the blood blackened Earth

Torn and shredded in defeat…

The fear laden face of Sol

Closes his hopeless eyes forever upon my towering countenance

Quaking with loathsome pride

I raise my voice and scream blackness into the rotting Heavens

Never-ending darkness collapses over the land

A newborn creature of eternal night

I stand huge and awful

My fell gloom so dense that I fair shine with intense anti-light

The very Earth trembles at my gaze

As I survey my evil, destructive creation

My dread chuckle rocks the mountains and the seas

With the despicable thirst of my insane vengeance ultimately slaked

I unclench my terrible fists and sigh…

Hoards of wet and slumberous flies pour, with deafening tumult

Into the cringing air, with the putrescence that is my grotesque
exhalation

They swarm hungrily into a swirling vortex

And burrow into the seething wound, that is your sad corpus

A sickening, popping, smacking is heard

Like that of raw, fatty meat dumped into the white hot coal of a
fiercely blazing bonfire

A damp, low, smothered grunting emanates from the roiling, swelling,
jiggling monstrosity that is the gory aftermath of your undeserved life

And your beautifully hideous death…

My demons rail with indignant rage

As I force them, snarling, like that aforementioned hound

Back down into the dark and hidden cavern, deep within my being

There to sit unrequited

until my return…

On the annual…

For…

A bone to pick…

And scatter…

To defecate upon your well deserved place of unhappy demise

And thus thoroughly insure eternal unrest and torment

For your utterly despised soul…

Until then…

Rest…

In…

My piss.

Available on <u>www.amazon.com</u> and <u>www.publishamerica.com</u>

In bookstores 12/17/07

NATURAL DRIVE
By
Charles Spencer

Outside, the predator felt his time had come.

If he could have returned the embrace of the darkness that concealed him that night like a conspirator, he would have. He took advantage of this like he did- with a primal, terrible satisfaction- the weakness of his prey. He felt his time had come, and in the darkness of night he cautiously approached the place where he knew his prey would be sleeping.

Inside, the guardian sensed something.

His head lifted and he looked into the darkness of his home which was comforting to him, and he wanted to return to sleep. But he knew with an instinct that something was wrong...there was a threat out there, somewhere, just beyond his ability to detect it. With nothing but those he loved in his mind, he tensed in preparation.

Outside, the predator was hungry.

He entered the inner perimeter of the place he had watched for hours, and continued closer to the home of his prey. He wanted to look around him at his surroundings, and he thought of other prey ignorant and asleep. But he had chosen this place, this singular place and knew it would hold certain reward...

With his hunger driving him, the predator continued ever

closer.

Inside, the guardian heard something approach from the outside.

His instinct proven right, he launched into motion silently any desire for sleep gone instantly. He made his way through the place that had been his home for years...he traveled through the familiar sights and smells that had always been a comfort to him. With nothing but those he loved in mind he prepared himself inwardly.

Outside, the predator's anticipation knew no boundaries.

He silently, methodically worked to gain entrance to the home of his prey. He took advantage of many things, like the often painfully inadequate means the homes of his prey were secured. He realized now would be no different from so many times before, for his efforts bore fruit within moments.

Inside, in familiar darkness, the guardian waited.

He had been trained and prepared on so many occasions for a moment like this. He had long ago resolved to live and die by any means for those he loved and swore at the most primal level to protect. He heard the threat gain entry, and he stiffened in anticipation. His ears were fully erect, locked on the threat he couldn't see yet. His lips peeled back from deadly teeth.

The predator quietly entered the home, more cautious than ever in spite of his hunger.

He always feared he would be caught, like he had been twice before by those who would deny him his prey. Unfortunately, there were so many ways, for better or worse, those who were a bane to him and his hunger proved to be inadequate. Their rule of law...their morality...such things meant nothing to one like him. And in many ways the means to guard against the likes of him meant little more than nothing, just paper trails and overcrowded prisons.

Yes, the predator had been caught twice before...but never as he hunted. No, he was caught in his very home and with his means to satisfy himself when he didn't hunt. The child porn he had a desire to collect from the Internet and other predators like him, seized. Those who executed the rule of law and morality didn't know the full weight of his terrible hunger.

They didn't know about the disappeared children, who satisfied the predator in the last frightening moments of their lives, and perhaps would never be found. And some of those who called themselves 'normal' were so foolish to believe he could be helped, could be rehabilitated. How can you teach someone, with any form of therapy, to not wish to eat? That was how primal his natural drive was. His hunger for sex with children was no different from the need another would have for food.

He had watched this home since he followed the mother and her two children here from the nearby mall. He had watched for hours, in spite of the sticky summer heat the darkness of night did little to cool. After realizing she had no husband and lived here alone with her son and daughter, he knew his hunger would be satisfied again soon enough.

He cautiously stepped into the main hall...

...and then he saw the shape, over thirty feet away, in the darkness of the hall.

It surprised him immediately, and for a moment he couldn't

discern exactly what it was in the darkness of this suburban home. The hall was darker than the room he left and there was much less ambient lighting, although he saw the bright crimson pinpoint of a smoke detector on the ceiling not much further away.

Then he heard the shadow growl.

The guardian knew nothing but cold rage the moment he saw the intruder.

The German Shepherd smelled the sudden fear in this threat who dared to invade the home of his master. The woman who loved and sheltered him as much as she did her children. The woman who had nurtured him since he was a pup. She had wanted him to stay inside, away from the intolerable heat of what later would be called the hottest day on record. But his rage was cold as ice as he growled at the threat that just entered the hall.

The guardian sensed what the predator would do just before the human went into motion.

The predator lifted his hand to reach under his jacket for his gun, but too late.

The German Shepherd exploded into a run.

The predator had no time to react, in these last frightening moments of his life, as the dog leapt for his throat.

A few rooms away, the woman woke with a start from the noise.

She quickly got out of her bed, wearing nothing but shorts and a long tee because the air conditioners barely countered the heat outside. She grabbed the baseball bat next to her bed, and her athletic form rushed to the bedroom next to her own, where her kids were sleeping. The mother looked into the open doorway, and realized with relief her children were still soundly asleep. The boy was snoring audibly, something she had overlooked in her fright.

The woman thought then of the one other in her home she loved, and she went into the main hall. She turned on the light above, and gasped reflexively.

She saw her dog, her guardian, sitting next to the prone form of a man who had his throat ripped out...the intruder was still twitching as his body began to figure out he was dead. The dog panted from his recent exertion, and his bloody mouth seemed to smile as he looked at his master with eyes full of total devotion. His tail wagged vigorously.

The woman quickly closed the distance to her guardian, knelt before him, and she wanted to hug the one who just protected her and her children. The blood on him made her think twice, though...but that quickly didn't matter as the German Shepherd bolted forward and began licking her face. She softly cried, "Huh!" She knew the big dummy had to be making a mess out of her, and a shower would be in order soon, but she stroked his fur in return and said softly, "Good boy...yes, you're a very, very good boy."

She looked at the dead man, and suddenly thought with dread what to do next about this. She thought fearfully that those who executed the rule of law and morality wouldn't see this the way she did. She knew that her guardian just obeyed his natural drive to protect her and her family. They might see him as a threat, as a killer, and she didn't want to imagine what might happen if they did. She didn't want anything to happen to her guardian. She would sooner die in his place.

Then she thought of her big back yard, where her guardian

buried his bones.

She started to wonder if she should call the police...

...or check her clock to see if she had time to bury this dead bastard before sunrise.

MIND TRAPPED
By
Nicole Rogers

A person's dreams are their secret world, they protect them as they sleep, but for Steven they are the ghosts that haunt him, he sleeps restlessly, the sun shines outside, but the light will not penetrate this dark room, nor will the warmth heat his heart and soul.

Three years ago he would have spent days like this is a class room, laughing and playing with friends; his biggest worry the exams; which to him would have seemed like a life time away. And now those simple exams *are* a life time away, they were in his life when his mother was, when his sister used to wake him in the morning and when he and his brother would throw water bombs at their parents.

He dreams of hot days like this in the past, the dreams always end the same way.

Like an old home made movie, he and his mate are inside, laughing in the kitchen getting a cold drink. Steven turns around and looks at the lounge room, nothing is out of place, but panic overtakes him. Something is wrong a white light shines across the floor in a strip. The door is open. In slow motion he runs reaching the door. He screams, but his voice is not heard over the screech of tires. He stops in the doorway and falls to the ground.

In his little room at home, where the sun shines outside, and the people he once called friends are at school, Steven wakes up, covered in sweat, breathing deeply. He has so many dreams like this every night, but no matter how many times he watches this distorted memory it still scares him. He did it, it didn't happen the way it does in his dreams, he killed her. His little sister Natalie, only four and he killed her. He's not alone in his room; he never is after his dreams. They stand there, they never say anything, but he knows they blame him, even if they don't show it. They are all dead and he killed every one of them.

His older brother Greg, arms crossed and pissed off at his little brother who wouldn't help him. He turns and leaves, just like he did the last time Steven saw him alive.

His sister, only four at the time, in one hand she holds a brown teddy bear that is almost as big as her, her other hand stretches up and holds her mothers hand. They look so alike. They have the same smile, big and warm, but while Natalie's eyes sparkle with joy, his mothers are full of sadness and pity, like the eyes of one who has had everything they love taken from them but refuses to blame anyone.

Natalie laughs, but the sound is hollow and heard only in Steven head. She lets go of her mothers hand and runs to the door, vanishing through the wood as if it wasn't even there. His mother stays, and holds Steven's gaze. She sits on the end of his bed, but she doesn't touch the sheets, the bed doesn't see the ghost like Steven does. She watches her youngest son, her eyes filling with tears, her mouth moves as if to say something, but no sound comes out. She reaches out with her hand, to place it on his cheek, but the closer her hand gets the more faded she becomes.

And then Steven is sitting alone in his room, his hand on his cheek. He wanted to put his hand on hers he wanted to feel the warmth of her touch. If he could take that last day back he would, but he knows he can't. He knows he killed her, even if he didn't do it with his own hands.

He gets out of bed and goes through the monotonous steps for getting ready for the day, but during breakfast he remembers how he was woken up in the night, to the sound of breaking glass.

He goes to his sister's room. There is still glass on the floor, he can feel it cut the soles of his feet, but he doesn't care. Nothing has been taken from the room, and his little sister's brown teddy bear stares at him from the top shelf.

"What?" he yells at the stuffed bear. "What do you want to blame this for me too?" He looks away from the bear, yelling isn't going to fix the window that is spread all across the floor in little shards. He leaves the room, making sure to close the door behind him. The glass is still cutting his feet, but he doesn't care. This pain is nothing compared to what he put his family through. He can live through this pain.

He gets some wood from the basement and takes it back to Natalie's room. He kneels, flinching as the glass cuts his knees. He closes up the window, making sure to block out the light. He's used to this. The houses windows are broken at least once a week.

Nothing is ever taken. No one wants to enter the house that's haunted by a murderer. That's what they all say he's heard them say it. They think he's dead, and if it wasn't for the pain that the glass cuts into him and the blood that covers the soles of his feet, he would believe that. After all he's not really living.

He leaves the room and calls the guy that fixes the windows for him.

"Hello, Window Fix here, how can I help you?" asked the voice of the receptionist.

"Hi, it's Steven again. Can I have a word to Max?" Steven's voice is croaky; he never uses it except when he calls stores to make orders for something.

"Sure thing, Steve, just one min. Okay, sweetie?" says the lady through the phone.

Steven hates the way she talks to him, she's married to Max and knows what happened to his family, but she talks to him like he's a little kid who's lost his parents in a shopping center. Her voice full of pity, but she should never pity him. He killed his family. He didn't lose them, he killed them.

"Hey Steve, what can we do for you today?" asks the rough voice that belongs to Max. For the last two and a half years now Max has been the one who comes down every week to fix windows the kids in the street have broken.

"It's my sister's window this time," explains Steven, his voice lost the life in it a long time ago, now it speaks as if disconnected to everything.

"I'll be down in 20 minutes, we have an opening. Just don't go into the room with bare feet. Okay, Steve?" Max's voice changes, becomes softer. He remembers how when he got there once the floor had been covered in blood. Steven had been lying curled up on the floor, broken glass pressed into his skin, slicing it open.

Steven's voice croaks, "Okay, thanks." He hangs up. He goes back to his sister's room; there isn't any blood on the floor this time. His knees are covered in sharp needles, but he got the job done fast so no blood fell to the ground.

He leaves the room and goes to the bathroom where he puts his feet under the cold water and washes away the blood and glass. The soles of his feet are covered in scars from the glass of all the other windows. The number of times he has cut his feet has made the skin tough, and while the water stings the cut, little blood falls.

Max arrives to fix the window, he lets himself in. Steven often leaves the door unlocked for him. Steven turns the television on, trying to drown out the noise that Max will start making soon.

Nothing on, damn day time TV. Steven slowly rises from his position on the couch, the curtains are all drawn the room is dark.

Food, he thinks to himself, *that's all I ever do, eat, eat, and more eating, nothing else to do.*

He walks to the fridge, but he's not hungry. He holds the door open and studies its contents without really looking at any of it. His thoughts aren't with the food, but off somewhere in a dream. The news flicks on in the other room. It brings him back to this world. He can just see the screen where he stands holding the fridge open. Scenes from the latest natural disaster flick across the screen. Devastation caused by earthquakes, floods, hurricanes, or tornadoes.

The world will fall to pieces, its people divided and trapped by their fear until it all ends, and it will all end, he thinks. It's a quote from a book he read once, but that was in a different life time.

Nothing new on, it's always the same. Devastation, war, famine, orphans, and then a small piece on how wonderful the world is and what good people are doing to save the world. Ha, people brought this on themselves, and I'm the crazy one. Ha...

The fridge door is still open and his mind wanders back to where he is. Studying the contents again Steven realizes he isn't hungry after all and shutting the door. He wanders back to the couch where he curls up in the fetal position and slowly slips into confused dreams.

His sister, sweet little innocent Nat is holding a gun. She is fully decked out in camouflage colors of the army. She say's something, but he doesn't listen. She slips into the cover of the trees surrounding them. His parents are by his side, "Watch her carefully," they call at him before running off.

"Nat" he screams after her. Too late she emerges from the tree line, gun fire, Steven squeezes his eyes shut. He knows she's dead, but he won't open his eyes. Gun fire everywhere. He hears her scream. The firing never stops or slows as if these people have endless amounts of ammo. "No, no, no," he says. It has to end sometime.

Someone calls but it's in the distance. A faceless voice is giving commands, but he won't go. Poor Nat.

"I'm sorry," he sobs to his parents who are walking away from him, dressed all in black. "I'm sorry." The tears roll down his face.

They are at a funeral. The army people are there, too. They fire seven shots of honor into the air.

Opening his eyes, it takes awhile to adjust to the dark. Steven can still hear gun shots, one round is close. Right behind him, even. He jumps. It's just a day movie. One of the old war movies.

Damned dreams, it was my fault.

He puts his hand on the couch for support, it is wet, wiping his eyes on the back of his sleeve. The TV is still going. *Where is that remote?* Turning the TV off, every thing goes quiet as if the world was put on mute. *Max must have finished fixing the window.*

Steven gets up and goes to check on the window. The money he left for Max is still on the bed. He didn't take it, but he hardly ever does.

Steven leaves the room, but as he shuts the door he hears something. Something in the room- a strange sound. Music, a song sung by a sweet voice.

For a moment his mind leaves his body. He stands with his hand on the door, and his eyes shut, remembering one day when he stood at this door. It was so long ago when he was still young and innocent. And from this room there came the sweetest sound he had ever heard before. The sound was so familiar to him that he had stopped and listened at the door.

The song ends in his mind and he watches as a young him opens the door and goes into the room, his mother had been singing to her new baby, her first daughter. She had sat Steven down then and told him of how she used to sing to him when he was a baby. She said that it had stopped him from crying and lulled him to sleep.

The memory fades behind his eyes and he is back at the door, listening to the song, but this song is so different to his mothers. This song is sad, it has no words, but the tune told a story of death and entrapment.

Steven opens the door and enters the room. The song stops and he shuts the door behind him. There is a small bird sitting on the bed. Quiet now, it watches the window. Steven walks towards it and it takes flight. It flies at the window, crashing headlong into the new glass. It must have flown in through the window in the morning before it was fixed. Steven rushes to the window, catches it, and holding on to it he pulls the curtains across the window, the room falls to darkness.

He turns the lights on low, and releases the bird. It doesn't see any escape anymore, so it flutters around the room until it finally lands on the wooden frame above the door. Steven perches carefully on the side of his sisters' bed, as if he was afraid he might break it. "Why would you ever want to go out there?" he asks the bird.

He doesn't expect it to answer, he isn't that crazy. He stares at the bird, and it looked back, almost pleadingly, like it was saying, *let me out*. Steven sits further onto the bed, leaning against the head rest. The bird takes flight again and lands on the cushions of the bay window.

It just stands there, then after a few moments it hops around and faces Steven. They just stand there, watching each other, curious of each other. Suddenly Steven starts to talk, his voice is cracked and strangled as if he wants to swallow what he is about to say. "You remind me of my sister, you know that?" he takes a deep breath and looks at the ceiling. "She's dead, and I killed her."

He swings his legs off the bed and slumps over, his body begins to shake. The bird just stands there. Steven looks up, takes another deep breath and looks over his shoulder at the bird. "She was only 4 years old when it happened, out there," he nods towards the window. "I was supposed to watch her, but she went outside, I left the door open. It's my fault."

He turns around to the bird that is still standing on the bay window. "I won't let the outside world kill you, too. I'll protect you, Nat." And with that Steven gets up and leaves the room, making sure the door is shut properly.

He isn't going to let Nat die again, not now when he has been given a second chance.

Nat had always been so much like their mother, she had loved the outside, and in the mornings you could always hear her humming the songs of the birds outside the window. She had hummed the same song as that bird sang, but it was different. When Nat sang it, it had been full of joy. The song had told how she was free, how cages would never be part of her life.

"I guess the bird would normally sing it the same way Nat would, but it'll see that I'm rescuing it. It's not trapped, it's free just like it used to be, but now it's safe too," Steven says out loud, more to the house than to himself.

That night as Steven sleeps he remembers the last time he saw his brother, how Greg had begged for help, explained that he owed a lot of money to the wrong people, Steven had turned him away.

"Solve your own problems," he had regretted the words as soon as he had said them. In his dream he tries to call his brother back, but he turns into the ghost that leaves his room every morning.

When he wakes up Steven sees the ghosts again, but he pushes them aside as he gets out of bed, choosing to ignore them. For a moment he pauses, as he swipes his hand through the air he actually expects to hit something more solid than a memory. Shaking his head at himself he goes straight to his sister's room.

"Nat," he calls. The bird is still asleep. He pulls the curtains open, the sky is still dark outside. He leaves the room and comes back with some bread. Breaking it up into smaller pieces he places it at the end of the bed, and he sits with his back against the pillows. There he sits talking to the bird that still sleeps.

"You know my brother, Greg? We used to be best friends," Steven explains. "Mum used to say he was a good kid, but he fell into the wrong crowed. That's when we started fighting. I heard mum cry at night. I told him to grow up, to stop being so selfish. He didn't though. At least I didn't think he did…" Steven's voice trails out, as he thinks back to what his brothers' friends had said to him after the funeral.

"Your brother was a good mate of mine, Steve. We've known each other since primary school. I knew something was up. He started doing drugs and that kind of shit. We had a falling out because of that, but you know what? He was really proud of you. He came to me three weeks back, said you'd set him straight, told him to grow up. Said it opened his eyes and that he was going to stop all this shit with drugs. He just had to pay the guy back then he'd be right. He was going make it up to you and you two would be best mates again. He said he'd make it up to everyone."

A ruffling of feathers brings Steven back to the present moment. "I didn't know that. I didn't know he was trying to get out. I thought he was buying more. He came to me for help, his last chance was me and

I turned him away. I was stupid, thought I was helping you know, tough love and all that, but I killed him."

Tears begin to drip down his face, "I could have saved him, but I condemned him to death instead. I have to carry that, I told mum what had happened. She said that I couldn't have done anything Greg had gotten in too far. She said all the money in the world would not have freed him, and he knew it. She said, *'They would have killed him even if he paid them off, he knew that, Steven. It's not your fault, you should know. He came to me that night, said he was going away for a while, but that we'd see each other again. But he knew he wasn't coming back, not in this life time. If he had ran they would have come after us, he faced them in order to keep us safe. Your brother saved your life.'"*

He repeats these words to the bird that still sleeps on the top shelf in the room, struggling to keep his voice steady. Dizzy headedness takes hold of him and he realizes he only ate breakfast yesterday. But now he is tired, sleep washes over him as little Natalie's room fades to darkness, to be replaced by a hazy dream.

It's the day little Natalie died. Steven watches as she runs out of the front door, and he stands in the doorway as she runs after her dolls pram, across the road. In slow motion a car comes around the corner, it clipped the path and skids across the road. It seems to speed up as it slams into his little sister.

But it is all so unreal. There is no noise, just the images. A strange sensation overcomes him as his memory of himself runs out of the door, his mouth screaming but with no noise. The person gets out of the car, panic written across his face, he is running late for an interview. But he won't make it to that interview, he didn't in real life and he wouldn't now.

There is no little body, no blood, and no broken glass on the windshield. It is as if he had never hit little Nat. Steven watches his memory unfold, he watches as if it isn't him running down the stairs. He watches as the road turns into a blur, and all that is left is him and the doorway, nothing beyond or below.

A tree takes shape next to the door. He remembers this tree, it had the prettiest flowers in spring, and Nat had worn them in her hair. But that tree has died since then, but in this dream it stands, strong and alive.

A little birdie sits in the branches. Steven looks into its eyes and saw his sister Nat. It begins to sing a mournful song of entrapment.

Steven wakes up, but the song, though more muffled in his dream, plays on in his head. But it isn't in his head, the sun has risen and the little bird sings to greet the new day. The song is full of joy at the sun finally rising, but it was also full of regret that she cannot be outside to fly into the rays and be warmed.

The little bird is standing on the cushions that lined the window again, and it is staring out the glass. It stays watching outside for some time. Neither of them makes any sound, but sits in silence, accepting that neither wants to talk. Both want to enjoy the warmth that was seeping into the room.

Steven feels the cold chill of night leaving him slowly. Warmth spreads inside his heart, a warm that he has not known for a long time. It is the warmth that comes when you let go of your dark secrets.

The Bird turns to look at him. Steven looks at the bird. He sees the pain of being trapped here in its little eyes. "Don't look at me like that, I'm protecting you," he says and turns away from the bird.

It flies across the room and lands on the bed. Steven stays perfectly still for a moment, not wanting to scare it away, but slowly he turns to face it again. Now silent tears escape his eyes, splashing down onto his shirt. He doesn't wipe them away nor try to blink to get rid of them. He allows them to freely fall from his eyes.

"I'm so sorry, Nat. I didn't mean for this to happen, honestly. If I could go back... but I can't. I know I can't."

The bird hops forward a bit and chirps, the sound fills the room with sorrow. It wants to be free, just like Steven wants to be free of this house and the memories in it. But he cannot go outside, he is trapped here forever.

Steven holds out his hands and examines them, front and back.

"They don't look like it, but these hands... they are covered in blood. First my brother, who I turned away, his blood stained them. Then my sister, who I was supposed to be watching, her blood stained them. Then my mother, the one that never blamed me, I killed them all. I should have been there for mum. She was the only other person suffering as much as me, the one that would have understood the tears.

"But you don't know what happened, do you? I suppose you weren't here to see it all happen. I locked myself away, refused to see people. My dad blamed me for their deaths; his son, his daughter, and all that was left was me... the mistake. *'Stop crying, you weak little shit! What the hell did I do to deserve you, hey??? Why didn't you help your brother? And then your sister! Christ, the kid can't even look after his little sister! What a useless piece of shit, get out of my face.'*

"That's what he said to me. That's all he had to say to me. Mum couldn't stand him after that, not when he started drinking. She kicked him out, but she couldn't stand being near me either so she left the house to me. She didn't want to live in silence. She came back and tried to talk to me, but I just ignored her. I rolled over and ignored her. God, I was such a little shit," Steven curls his knees up to his chest and wraps his arms around them.

He stays like that for a long time. He takes deep breaths, wanting to say more about what happened, but steadying himself first, as the room swims in his blurred vision.

"She used to leave food at the door for me every week. She'd come in every couple of days to talk after work. She wasn't coping, either. I think looking after me meant she still had something to do, something that involved life rather than just death that surrounded her."

Steven watches the bird for a moment. It has eaten some of the bread and now it just sits watching him. It looks as if it is trying to reach out to him with its thoughts, explain something that Steven doesn't understand. It chirps at him and jumps forward slightly.

Steven continues talking, taking a deep breath before he begins again. "The last time I saw her, she was in this room. I came in and sat next to her, she turned to look at me. Her eyes were red from crying. Her skin was so pail. I can still see that look on her face, one of pure desperation. I even remember what she said, it was so long ago but I remember every word.

"'I've lost all my children, they are all dead. I've lost my husband, my job, my baby girl, my oldest son, and now I've lost the only one left to me, they'll never come back to me.'

"After she said that I just sat their, I didn't know what to think, she got up and left and I sat here. Here on this bed and I thought, maybe I have died. Maybe I never woke up this morning, but I know that's not true. She had lost me, lost me to grief. I found out later that I was the last person she spoke to. She went home, took sleeping pills and got into the bath. She never woke up. She died because I refused to talk, it could have saved both of us."

He takes a deep breath again, steadying himself, his emotions draining him of his strength.

"Food kept appearing in the kitchen. Monday mornings. I thought maybe it was all just a bad dream. I thought that she wasn't really dead and I could still save her. Then I woke early one morning to see who it was. As the door clicked unlocked, I really thought I'd see her again, but it wasn't her. She really was dead. It was my father. He saw me and froze on the spot. He put the food down and began to walk out the door again. I called out for him to stop. Do you know what he said to me?"

He looks at the bird, half expecting it to actually know. *"'You're not my son, my kids have all died. I'm doing this for my wife, because I owe that much to her at least.'* That's all he said to me. Then he left. He still blames me, and I get that. After that I don't get up early anymore, I sleep in. I know she's dead, they all are."

The bird chirps louder and jumps back onto the bed. Its feathers ruffle like it is angry or it's trying to scare off a predator. It holds Stevens gaze and chirps again.

"I know, it's been years since mum died, years of locking myself up in here. Years of self hatred and depression. Years of waisted life. Mum didn't lose her other baby, I was still there, but I've been dying for so long. And now… and now I'm about to put you through what I put myself through."

Steven sighs. "Sure the world out there is dangerous at times, but look at me, I might as well be dead."

Fresh tears well in his eyes and threaten to fall, but Steven holds them in place. "I've been feeling sorry for myself for too long. I can't expect you to live like this, your eyes and songs talk of morning space. Of fresh air and of the bright sun. Just like Nat's songs used to, she had the same free spirit. I could never have kept her locked away, she would have lived, but her spirit would have died."

Steven gets out of the bed and goes to the window. He looks outside and turns to see the little bird standing on the bed watching him. Pure joy in its eyes, he picks it up, but it doesn't struggle like last time, he walks down the hallway and stops at the door. For a moment he just stands there, waiting for something to happen, his hand reaches out without him noticing and it opens the door. His other hand releases the bird, but it doesn't fly away, it just stands on his hand watching him.

It chirps its thanks and goes. Steven stands in the door way with the sun against his face. Fresh air rushes into his lungs and a sweet melody reaches his ears, one of freedom, and of a strong spirit that will live forever. Steven takes a deep breath, pictures his family is his mind. They are all smiling at him now, proud that he has finally released his secrets. He takes his first step in years over the threshold. As he walks down the path his brother walks at his side, their feet falling at the same time, he claps Steven on the back. A small child appears at his side. She reaches out and takes hold of his hand. He looks down and they smile at each other. The small child giggles, in her other hand she holds her teddy bear and her mother walks at her side.

They are finally free, a screech of tires.

They are free, and the bird will sing their song forever.

13 HUMAN SOULS

VISIT
WWW.GEOCITIES.COM/
THIRTEENHUMANSOULS

BRANDON LAYNG'S
EZINE FEATURING
SOME OF THE BEST
FLASH FICTION IN THE
WORLD

THE WATCHER AT THE GATE

By

Alexander Rivera

She could not recall the exact moment at which her trepidation at the sight of the watcher at the gate had turned to outright paralyzing fear.

It could not be encapsulated into any one particular thing, or crystallized into a certain given moment of time. It was not specifically the grey-stone snake-slit eyes that seemed to follow her wherever she went, nor the mouth full of icicle point teeth around which Stacy could swear a snarl would form at the footfalls of each passer-by.

In retrospect, she believed that, had she viewed this apartment block during twilight hours prior to signing the lease she would have never dared to venture near the place ever again.

But it had been broad daylight when she had first set eyes upon it and the imposing stone structure atop the right-hand entrance pillar had looked anything but sinister; just another old stone statue on another square brick column dividing the black metal railing from the entrance to the building.

It had not seemed like something alive, like something that could extend its wings and bring them sweeping down with an air-slicing ferocity as it perched, standing sentinel at the gate, under an opaque witness moon.

The thing that had struck her as odd at her first sight of the statue was the fact that there was only one of them. The majority of buildings in this part of the city, or anywhere else for that matter, generally had two gargoyles guarding the exterior, if any.

But, as time passed and with each journey home, her heart would begin to pulse and quicken, like it was trying to break free of her rib cage, as she would hurry past the brown-brick square tower upon which it rested. When she could see it, when it was in full view, she could convince herself she was fine, but as it slipped out of her line of vision, so her body began to react detrimentally to her perceptions, extra-sensory or otherwise.

There was the thumping in her chest, the film of sweat that would form on her skin, the raising on the hairs on the back of her neck and the unsettling feeling that would take root in the pit of her stomach.

Out of the corner of her eye, in her mind's eye, she would see its giant bulldog head turn, and angle towards her, contemplating her every movement. She would hear its low rumbling growl and the grind of stone on stone, like the noise of a tablet being lifted from a sarcophagus, as it rose on its haunches and prepared to descend. She would see the shadows cast by its huge wingspan as it flexed, expanded and primed for attack.

Except, these things never happened. It crouched perpetually motionless on the pillar, front legs extended between its rear paws, bolt upright, lifeless head staring silently into eternity with eyes of stone that never flinched and teeth that were constantly bared but, with wings furled, blocking out even the brilliant sunlight to those who walked beneath its gigantic shadow.

It was so big, she thought. Most of these types of statues were a couple of feet at most but this could not have been less than eight feet tall from the single thumb-claw at the tip of its wings to the dagger blades on the tip of its paws.

Stacy had asked her landlord, a small, portly and balding man in his fifties (aren't they all) where it had come from but he could tell her only that it had been there where he bought the property and that he did not know much else except that it hadn't been there when the place was built. And it had been this hulking monolith which had troubled her more than the disquieting history of the house prior to her moving in.

Apparently, the tenancy of the previous residents, a couple, had come to a premature demise when the husband had 'bludgeoned' his wife with a heavy, blunt object.

(Why people took gleeful delight in the descriptive aspects of such tales as the landlord who had recounted this story, she never had nor would ever understand).

"Interestingly enough," the landlord had told her, and in the imagination of her recollections he was wringing his hands. "They found the apartment covered in near equal amounts of their blood, officially it was recorded as a murder-suicide. But his body was never found. You can check that if you like," he had concluded with a knowing nod and a smirk. She never had.

And now, for how long she could not remember, although it

seemed like it could have been years despite the fact that she had stayed here only two months, the peaceful walk home from her office transformed into an exercise in holding her nerve at the moment she turned onto the Catalpa street block of the Ravenswood district of Chicago where she stayed.

Had there been a back entrance for her to go to she would have taken it, but the building adjoined the identical complexes on either side and, on the opposite block the same thing happened. It would have meant her entering on the opposite side of the street, crossing two back yards and one hedge, all for a fear she suspected might be in her mind. She had contemplated this often, as she sat, dressed primly in her pin-stripe business suit, hair in a bun, at her desk in the office of the accounting firm where she worked idling away another long, meaningless day.

But she was able to put these imaginings to the back of her mind. Work kept her busy, most of the time. Stacy was successful enough, and probably should have thought of moving onward and upward, except for the fact that she was comfortable. Comfortable, that was, until the walk home and the creeping doubts about the watcher at the gate began to surface.

On this particular day, she switched off her computer, packed up her things, walked to the Red-line 'L' that took her most of the way home and then steadied herself as she got off the train and prepared to walk the last ten minutes home.

Nothing had happened before and there really was nothing to fear. Except, however, tonight the danger was real. She had seen a man, dressed in dark clothing and wearing a woolen hat low over his brow, standing on the corner of the street for the last two evenings and had thought nothing of it when he had not moved as she walked by. She had toyed with the idea that he might have been watching her but then thought better of it.

However, now he was doing more than watching. He was following the vapor trails of her scent. She was sure of it. It was at the exact moment she realized she was being followed that she understood why people in trouble would quicken to a brisk walk, as she was doing now, before doing the sensible thing and breaking out into an all out, arms flailing, lungs heaving run.

Some part of the pursued, the prey, wants still to believe that it is not being stalked and makes any attempt to deny the impending terror, even fleeting.

When Stacy heard those footsteps from behind her quicken from speed-walk to sprint and urged her legs to follow suit – she could make the door before he got to her, could keep her feet and hope he sprawls on the rain slicked street – she felt betrayed to discover her feet had filled with a heavy lead of her imagining.

A cloud drifted across the moon and cast her stone behemoth into the blackest darkness in a weird kind of eclipse as she staggered towards the safety of the front door. This time the thud of footsteps in chase was real, the breath of the nape of her neck was not from an imagined monster and the heart-bursting panic was not to be in vain.

In lieu of the frantic sprint of escape her mind hoped erroneously her body could achieve, Stacy fixed her effort on exhaling a scream. A scream of panic, of hope, the supplication of fear, of pleaded rescue, of all the images burning through her brain in those final seconds. At first her lungs would not obey and she choked down cold, moist, fresh November air. She gagged and wheezed and out of the silence she could not break, footsteps came closer, breathing became heavier and an actual shadow of imminent violence overwhelmed her. She begged her lungs to give her the air to let out one last shriek of defiance - and then there was a cacophony.

Her fear turned to joy as the silence was obliterated by an earth shattering symphony of noise, a crashing so loud as to pierce her ears and ring in her brain. But then she realized there was no sound emitting from her fear-frozen lungs and throat but the sharp intake of breath and the stuttering gasp of someone who can't get air to where it needs to be.

Turning to the source, Stacy saw her assailant enveloped in a flurry of violence. Laser red eyes gleamed in the dark, silver fangs shimmered and sliced in the glistening moonlight and now leathery wings flapped over the stricken man, concealing him from sight. The growling Stacy had long become accustomed to be replaced by a strange slurping sound.

It was this, more so than anything that caused her to pass out.

She woke up shortly after to see the street packed with police cars, ambulances and fire trucks. Firefighters were using a standard hoist device to lift the fallen statue off the badly mangled victim it had apparently collapsed on.

At the hospital Stacy was checked over and allowed to return home the next day after spending the night there. She was told that it looked like the weight of the statue had caused it to overbalance, that it had probably been shifting imperceptibly for years before it had become too much for the pillar it was on to sustain, and that it was a freak accident that that man had been standing under it when it had finally given way. They were still trying to explain his blood loss, however, because it seemed that he didn't have much at all left, even though there was little at the scene.

"That house has a bad vibe," her petite, neat uniformed nurse told her, "I remember the night they brought that woman in, all beat up after her husband had taken an ashtray to her. That place is bad, bad news."

Despite this, Stacy continued to reside there to this day and, though she has had no problems since, the thing that struck her as strange is this: though the statue was back where it belonged atop the right-hand entrance pillar, no-one, not the council, the landlord, the police, the firefighters or residents of the building, will admit to having replaced it.

And so still it sits, motionless, silently, waiting...

WORD WEAVERS
COME WEAVE WORDS OF WONDER WITH US

"Weaving webs of words to enlighten, inspire and entertain!"

Come Join Authors Jennifer L. Miller, M. L. Chesley, Dave Rex, and Cassandra Lee at:

http://www.myspace.com/weaversofwords

Word Weavers is a Diverse writing Group that offers lots of Support and of course a lot of Exposure! Whether you write, read, or just enjoy the company of good people, you'll find a niche with this group!

Word Weavers offers Four Day Features Writing Excerpts Short Story Anthologies and our Exclusive Word Weavers Trading Cards!

Stop by to see how to get yours today!

VISIT OUR FRIENDS ONLINE

APARTMENT J

By

Gabrielle S. Faust

Howling. A warped, demented, feline yowling had caused the floorboards and walls of Izzy's one bedroom apartment to vibrate for the past hour, echoing down through the thin layers of decaying wood and plaster from the unit above. Ever since Ms. Adams had moved in upstairs, as soon as the clock struck midnight the hellish noise, as if dozens of cats tore at one another's throats, would begin, the sound of their nails digging into the wood floors as they raced from one room to another maddening in its desperation. Izzy sat on the floor of her bedroom gripping the sides of her head as she stared up at the ceiling sure that she would soon begin to see cracks in the drywall. She had complained to the management team on several occasions, but to no avail. Just as with all of the repair issues in the ten-unit complex, their response was "move if you don't like it".

"Goddamn it," Izzy growled, unable to take the screams a moment longer. "This has got to stop or I'm going to fucking lose it."

She scrambled to her feet. Barefoot and muttering to herself, she stomped up the two flights of termite-ridden wood stairs to the second floor landing. Her footsteps echoed loudly off the cracked plaster walls. She wondered, as she reached the top, how the neighbor across from apartment "J" could stand the sound, but then, perhaps the girl that lived there was simply able to tune it out. Some people were highly adept at selective hearing. Izzy took a deep breath, not relishing the idea of yet another bizarre encounter with the unfriendly, spinster neighbor. There in the dull yellow glow of the hallway lamp she pounded the peeling white paint of Ms. Adam's door with her fist. The howling suddenly died away. Izzy frowned, feeling the fine hairs on the backs of her arms bristle at the strange absence of sound. Several moments passed, but the door remained closed. Izzy pounded on it again, the blows booming in the tiny corridor.

Metal scraping upon metal screeched as the several locks up on the interior of the door were pulled away and the door opened a crack, the top chain still in place. Ms. Adams' pinched face glared at her silently from within.

"Hello, Ms. Adams. I'm sorry to disturb you again, but you have to make those cats of yours stop." Izzy's voice was trembling slightly as she attempted to remain calm.

"Cats will do what cats will do," Ms. Adams replied bluntly, her eyes unblinking as she stared up at Izzy. "They don't listen to me."

Izzy took a deep breath as she felt her pulse begin to race with anger. "I know, but the sound is really awful. I can't sleep with all of the-"

The door slammed shut leaving Izzy alone again in the hall. Izzy felt the dam restraining her rage burst. With a small shriek she pounded on the door again. "Ms. Adams, you get out here right now! This is bullshit! You can't make me live like this! If I hear one more peep out of you or your damned cats I will call the police! Do you hear me in there, you freak? I will call the police and have you and your mangy animals hauled out of this building!"

There was no reply. Izzy was shaking. She ran her hands through her long, brown hair. The sleep deprivation was starting to wear on her nerves. She stomped back down the stairwell and out the screened door. Across the courtyard the lights in Maxine's apartment glowed welcomingly from behind heavy living room curtains. Izzy knocked on her front door.

Maxine answered, her wild curly hair frizzing out in every direction from the humidity of the summer night. "Hey. What's up?" She answered sleepily and then, noticing Izzy's distraught expression, added, "You okay?"

"Do you have a smoke I could bum?" Izzy asked, still feeling like she could claw her way out of her own skin.

"Yeah, hold on. I'll come out and smoke with ya." Maxine disappeared inside for a moment before reappearing with a pack of American Spirits and a couple of Orange Crush soda cans. She handed one to Izzy as they walked out to the rusted metal lawn furniture in the center of the muddy courtyard.

"Let me guess." Maxine said as she settled herself into one of the chairs around a large table. "The cat lady is up to her tricks again."

"Yes!" Izzy breathed in her seat as she lit a cigarette. "I don't know what I'm going to do. I would hate to call animal control because you know that will only make the situation worse, but it's really creepy. I'm almost worried that she's hurting those animals up there."

"You think they're in heat or something?" Maxine asked, blowing smoke out in front of her. It lingered in the still, moist air as if unsure of where to go next. "Maybe she's breeding a certain kind. I've heard that cats make some strange sounds when they're breeding."

"Now, that's a disturbing idea," Izzy replied with a strangled laugh. "As if I had trouble getting to sleep before, now the image of dozens of cats fucking above my bed is going to be burned into my brain."

"Sorry," Maxine laughed. "I don't know what to tell you. These places are just dumps. We really need to move."

"I know, but I can't afford to. At least not for a while longer." Izzy took another drag. "It's just a shame. Of all of the apartments in this town, I have to pick the one that's cursed. I've had nothing but bad neighbors above me since I moved in. I swear it's built directly over a portal to Hell!" She pointed to her ground floor apartment nestled in the corner of the building. Shaking her head, she stared up at the dull glow emanating from behind Ms. Adams' curtained windows above. "I just wish I knew what exactly was going on up there."

"We could take a look," Maxine said.

Izzy looked at her, frowning. "What do you mean?"

Maxine pointed to the porch overhang that ran beneath second floor windows. "There's a ladder around back. We could climb up there and peek in her windows."

Izzy pulled a grimace. "I don't know about that. What if someone saw us? Besides, I doubt if that roof would hold us. It's mostly rotten."

"Nah." Maxine replied. "I've seen the maintenance guys up there before working on AC units and stuff. Hey, I bet Cooper would let us in sometime when she's out. I'm pretty sure he's still in charge over there at that subcontractor place the slumlords use."

"Hmmm…" Izzy hummed softly as she thought. "You really think he'd do that? Isn't that illegal?"

"Yeah, it is, but Cooper owes me one." Maxine winked slyly and smiled as she took a sip of soda. "I'll give him a call tomorrow."

• • •

That Saturday afternoon Maxine came over to Izzy's apartment with Cooper in tow. Lanky and tan and barely out of his teens, Cooper was the savoir of the Peach Tree Palace residents, tending to the repairs which the landlords stubbornly denied.

"Sounds quiet up there," he remarked as they stood in Izzy's tiny living room and glanced up at the ceiling.

"She's gone. Left about a half hour ago," Izzy replied, unconsciously wringing her hands. For some reason she felt ill at ease about entering Ms. Adam's apartment without her permission.

"Guess we'd better get moving, then," Maxine said and reached for the front door.

"How long do you think she'll be gone?" Cooper asked as they climbed the stairs.

"She usually leaves for a couple of hours in the afternoons on the weekends. Not sure where she goes, but it seems pretty routine," Izzy replied, watching Cooper fish through his key ring, the metal keys jangling noisily in the shafts of afternoon light that filtered in the triple paned windows to the right of the landing between the apartments.

"Well, that should give us enough time for a quick look around." He found the key and slipped it into the top deadbolt lock. "I tell ya, I wouldn't do this for just anyone, ya know." He glanced over his shoulder at Maxine.

"I really appreciate it," Izzy said, giving him a quick hug from the side as he opened the doorknob lock.

"Yeah, yeah," he muttered as he pushed the door open.

Izzy ducked around Cooper through the open door. Inside the curtains were still drawn. The thick odor of dust and moldy fabric was stifling, the silence heavy, as if the shadows held their breath as the three entered.

"Man, and I thought I had an empty apartment," Cooper muttered under his breath as he cautiously followed the women inside.

"Yeah, this is very strange." Maxine said quietly.

The living room was nearly barren with the exception of one high-backed antique armchair and a low round wooden table set in the center of the spacious room. The walls, a dull gray the color of overcast skies, were bare. From where she stood, Izzy could see that the dining room was bare as well, the one window covered in the same thick black curtains as the ones that adorned the living room.

"So, where are all of these cats you've been hearing?" Maxine asked, folding her arms over her chest and rubbing her upper arms with her hands as if to ward off a chill.

"What?" Izzy replied quietly as she stared at the strange chair studying the ornately carved wood and velvet lined seat.

"The cats? The yowling, screaming, breeding cats? Where are they?" Maxine's voice was starting to take on the grating edge it got when her anxiety attacks were about to set in.

"I don't know," Izzy replied quietly. The apartment was eerily vacant. Izzy's heart began to race a bit faster and the sudden urge to flee the building clawed at her spine until it itched, but she couldn't leave just yet.

"I'm going to check the bedrooms." She started for the dark, narrow hallway towards her right when she heard Maxine gasp behind her.

"Holy Moses," Maxine hissed.

"What?" Izzy snapped, her nerves frying beneath her skin, and whirled back around to face her friend.

Maxine answered by pointing at the floor near the baseboards. "Are those claw marks?" Her eyes were saucers of pale green and black. Slowly she walked towards the wall. "What the fuck's been up here?" The deep, rough grooves in the wood ran all the way around the room in a two-foot wide track as if something had been running frantic, terrified laps.

"Coop, has this always been like this?" She knelt down and touched the wood with trembling fingers.

"Hell, no!" Cooper squatted down next to Maxine to study the marks. "This place was just fine before she moved in. I inspected it myself." He stood up, shaking his head, and ran his fingers through his dark hair, muttering obscenities beneath his breath. "This damage is irreparable. They'll have to rip out the whole floor and replace it. The landlords aren't going to be happy about this."

Izzy's heart began to race, dread slowly raking its razor talons down her spine. "Something's telling me we should leave now." She turned and started for the door.

"You okay, Izz?" Maxine asked, tearing her gaze away from the grooves in the floorboards.

Izzy paused at the doorway, her hand on the molding. "Yeah," she replied, unconvincingly. "I think I've just seen enough for one day."

● ● ●

That night, after Izzy returned home from running her weekend errands, she found her answering machine blinking another spiteful message from her landlord. Izzy poured herself a heavy glass of cabernet, leaving the bottle open on the blue tiled counter in the kitchen, and pressed the little plastic play button again.

Mrs. Aberdeen's voice crackled in a bitchy, smoke-hoarse snarl from the round speaker. "Like I told you before; if you don't like you are more than welcome to move."

"I swear. Someone should put a hex on that woman and be done with it." Izzy sank into the old armchair next to the front door, propping her feet up on the coffee table as she stared at the wobbling ceiling fan slowly turning above.

It was quiet upstairs at the moment, though she knew Ms. Adams was home from occasional creaking of the floorboards as she walked across the living room from time to time. A cold, sickening dread coiled tightly in Izzy's stomach causing the wine to curdle like sour milk, yet she kept drinking.

Who are you, old woman? She thought silently as her gaze traveled over the cracks in the sagging, painted drywall. *Maxine and Coop must think I'm completely insane. But I'm not, am I, Ms. Adams?*

Izzy felt trapped more than ever now that she had seen the disturbing, barren interior of the apartment above. Even if she called the cops once the yowling began again, and she knew that it eventually would, what would they do if they found nothing up there? Would they haul Izzy away? Could Ms. Adams press charges for harassment? Izzy was unsure of what the law could entail in such a situation and did not savor the idea of making a horribly uncomfortable situation far worse. After an hour of silent contemplation and another glass of wine she decided to give peaceful negotiation one last try.

Setting her glass on the edge of the coffee table Izzy slipped on her shoes and left her apartment. At the top of the stairs, she drew a deep breath to steady herself. The wine had tempered her anxiety somewhat, but now as she stood before the peeling white paint of Ms. Adams' door, she began to feel her pulse race again. Chewing nervously on her bottom lip, she slowly raised her fist and rapped quietly upon the wood. A long moment passed in tense silence and she thought briefly that perhaps Ms. Adams would refuse to answer the door once she saw Izzy through the peephole. She raised her fist once more, but before she could knock again, she heard the familiar sound of chains being slid back and locks being turned.

The door opened a crack revealing darkness beyond and Ms. Adams' pale, heavily lined face. She said nothing as she stared at Izzy.

Izzy felt her throat tighten, "Hello, Ms. Adams. I wanted to apologize for yelling the other night."

Ms. Adams said nothing.

"I was hoping that perhaps we could sit down and talk? Maybe work something out?" Izzy's voice came out as a squeak as her instincts screamed silently within her to run back down the stairs and barricade herself in her apartment. Her palms had begun to sweat and she folded her arms across her chest, tucking them against her sides.

Ms. Adams regarded her coolly, her eyes narrowing as she tilted her head to one side. Izzy felt as if her soul were being read silently and against her will.

"I suppose that might be possible," Ms. Adams said quietly.

Izzy gulped painfully, releasing the breath that had become stuck in her lungs as she had waited.

"Why don't you come in?" Ms. Adams opened the door slightly.

Izzy hesitated a moment too long. Her jaw tensed till it ached, she wished she had just let it go and taken Mrs. Aberdeen's advice about moving. Outside in the driveway below, she heard the tires of one of the other tenants' cars leaving.

"What's wrong?" Ms. Adams hadn't blinked in at least a minute, her mouth, set in a hard thin line, curling at the edges in a sour facsimile of a smile. She opened the door a bit further.

Izzy shook her head, forcing a smile of her own. "N-nothing. It's just been a very long day." She stepped across the threshold.

Inside the room was lit only with the glow of several tall red candles set into a simple candelabra in the center of the round table. Though the hum of an AC unit was strangely absent, the temperature of the room was frigid. Izzy felt goose bumps prickle along her bare forearms as her eyes darted nervously about.

Ms. Adams passed beside her and sat down in the chair in the corner. A large leather-bound book lay upon the table in front of her. "I'm sorry I don't have more seating," she said quietly. "I don't get many visitors."

"Oh, it's alright." Izzy said, trying to sound nonchalant, frozen in her place near the front door. She rubbed her forearms to ward off the chill. She realized she had instinctually begun to stare at the claw marks in the wood floor and quickly returned her gaze to meet Ms. Adams'. Again, the apartment was eerily absent of the cats she had heard night after night.

Ms. Adams folded her hands in her lap and regarded Izzy coolly, "So, tell me what is bothering you?"

Izzy frowned slightly, confused. "Um, well, I wanted to talk to you about your cats... But it appears they're gone? May I ask what happened to them?" She swore she could smell incense burning somewhere in the complex over the heavy scent of melting wax and fire and something else, something sharp and coppery and pungent that hadn't been present earlier that day.

Ms. Adams was quiet for a moment before answering. "My dear, I fear you are mistaken. I've never owned cats."

"What?" Izzy felt her anger begin to bubble up past her fear. "Yes, yes you do! You have them. You told me the other night to my face about how 'cats will be cats' or something like that!"

Ms. Adams slowly stood and approached Izzy, "I think you're confusing me with someone else. Feel free to look for yourself." She gestured to the dark hallway that led to the bedroom beyond. "This place is empty. It's just me and my old bones rattling around this place."

Damn it! What kind of crazy game is this witch playing with me? Izzy thought with a hiss. "Maybe I'll do just that!" She snapped and turned away, charging down the hallway to the rooms that lay somewhere in the darkness beyond.

As she stomped down the narrow corridor, the sharp scent she had noticed moments before began to increase until she could taste it in the back of her mouth, heavy and rancid above a thicker perfume of nauseating sweetness. She shivered involuntarily. Izzy flicked the light switch to the first bedroom to her left several times, but nothing happened. Carefully, with only the light from the single parking lot florescent pouring through naked windows on the north and west walls, she quickly inspected the room. Flinging open the closet doors she fully expected to see cages and cages of crated starved animals, but nothing. Feeling frustrated tears beginning to brim in her eyes, blurring her vision, she turned and ran to the second room across the hall, the one situated directly over her own bedroom.

Izzy skidded to a halt three feet into the room. The walls were red, streaked wildly as if painted hastily with a single brush. In places Izzy was sure she could see the imprint of a palm or smeared fingers. With the exception of a low, round wood table, similar to the one in the living room that squatted in the center of the room, the room was as barren as the rest of the apartment. Upon the table burned five black candles, equidistant from one another about its edge. Izzy could feel herself trembling. Her mind raced in a terrorized panic. *Oh, my god! What the hell is this place? I shouldn't have come here. I knew I shouldn't have come here. Why did I come back? I should have just moved.*

She became aware of the fact that her back was still to the door and jumped forward into the room, whirling around to face the pitch-black hallway behind her. Down the corridor strange sounds had begun to wind, a low moaning and creaking like fierce storm winds through barren branches. Izzy glanced at her watch; midnight, the time when she had always heard the sounds begin.

She forced words from her lips, "Ms. Adams? Are you out there? Ok, I get it. Ha, ha! Game's over. I'll leave you alone, I promise." Her body was shaking uncontrollably as she found herself walking backwards across the room.

The only response was the loudening of the sound, the moaning writhing and warping into the maddening yowling and shrieking she had become so accustomed to, though it took on a whole new dimension without the layers of drywall to separate her from it.

Her eyes darted around the room, looking frantically for some sort of escape. She grabbed hold of the knob to one of the French doors to the closet and pulled it open. Gasping, she staggered back at the atrocity she saw hanging inside. From large silver hooks hung what appeared to be the empty skins of human beings, wet husks without their skeletons, their clothes still stuck to the gore-streaked, crumpled messes of flesh. The walls and doors were stained deep red, flies and maggots writhing in a white and black carpet upon the floor below.

Izzy felt bile rise in her throat, tears streaming down her face as she screamed and staggered away, whirling back towards the door. She started to run for the doorway only to realize that something now approached. Its footsteps heavy echoes of black thunder. The creaking tear of claws slowly digging through splintering wood inched closer and closer, the snarling howls becoming deafening. Izzy pressed her hands against her ears as she shook uncontrollably, watching the silhouette of the twisted demonic creature in the hallway seep up out of the shadows, backlit by the candles in the far room. She screamed as it lunged for her heart...

A WALK IN THE SUN

By

Jim Shifflett

He died yesterday. It is a loss that I can not quite relay to you. I sit here in the darkness of the parlor staring at his mortal remains. Memories flood my mind of days long ago. Days of his youth. Holding his hand in mine as we would take a walk in the sun through the park. It was his favorite place to spend time with me. We would talk. He would talk actually and I would try to answer his questions to the best of my ability or interject a few comments to help him understand the world around him.

Sometimes we would feed old stale bread to the ducks and geese by the pond. He would laugh and then run and jump in my arms when one of the geese would get a bit too close.

He was always amazed by how the wind would blow through the leaves in the trees. He would say that they, the trees, were talking to each other and that sometimes he could hear their voices and what they were saying. I would smile with the thought that maybe it was true.

I would watch him as he took to the air on the playground swing set and wonder how far in life he actually would fly. With his curiosity, I didn't think that the sky would even be the limit with him.

Yes, I know, I had a grandfather's prejudice, but he really was one of those people that would light up any darkness, be it within someone's soul or a shadowed room. It saddens me that this darkness I brood in now cannot be shed with his brightness.

You know, the last time he saw me, (that he knew of anyway), was when he was about five years old. I must have been around forty-five or so. He and his mother- my daughter- were living with us while her husband was serving a tour in Afghanistan after the whole 9/11 mess. I remember saying good-bye to him before I left that morning. I didn't realize then how permanent that would be.

I was leaving on a trip to visit some family members down in southeast Texas for a few days. He cried as I hugged him good-bye and didn't want to let go of me. I assured him I would be back in a few days time and that I would take him to the park when I got back.

Even now, all these years later, it still feels like I lied to him. I gave him back to his mom and crawled into the car. I wish I hadn't now.

The trip itself was pretty uneventful most of the way. However, shortly after dusk had officially given up the ghost to night on some Texas back road near Maud, my car began having trouble.

I pulled over on the edge of the road, pulled my flashlight out of the glove box, and got out to see if I could find the problem under the hood. Right away I felt something was wrong. There was no noise. No sounds of the night bugs usually found in the area. No wind blowing.

Nothing.

Nothing, except the sound of my heart beating. It seemed to be picking up its pace as I stood there. I looked around the area I was stranded in but could see very little except what was in the faint light of my flashlight and that was mainly tall grass and a few trees on the sides of the road and the road itself. It was a very dark night. No moon and very few stars.

After a few moments of fighting my own paranoia, I popped the hood of the car and began investigating the engine compartment for what was wrong. That is the moment when my life would be changed forever.

Life. What a strange word defined by a strange world. Life and live.

Anyway, it was at that moment life became something more, (or less), than living.

As I was bent over the engine, something hit me from the left side and knocked me down into the road. My ribs felt like I had just been struck by one of those hammers they use at carnivals. The game where people try to hit that little platform that sends up whatever that thing is that rings the bell at the top of the post.

My head, from the impact of the fall on the road, definitely felt like there were bells going off in it. My glasses had been knocked off my face and were lost in the darkness.

I had lost my flashlight in the assault as well. It was rolling back and forth on the ground and in the rocking light I could see something that my mind had trouble understanding right at that moment. It was a young and very beautiful woman. The kind of beauty that photographers try to capture in those model magazines that my wife would sometimes look at when we were at the check-out counter at the Piggly Wiggly.

She wore a tattered white dress with what appeared to be some kind of flower pattern on it (perhaps daffodils) and nothing on her feet. But something was wrong with her. She seemed off. Untouchable. And I don't mean prom queen to the science nerd untouchable. I mean untouchable in a way that you felt as if you would die (or at least want to die) if you did touch her. Made my stomach turn.

It may have been a trick of the rolling flashlight, but it actually seemed as if the darkness was either moving right through her or out of her. Wasn't sure which.

As I lay there looking up at her, she moved towards me. At least, I think she did. I did not see her step forward, but she was definitely closer to me than when I first noticed her. Each time the flashlight rolled she appeared closer. My heart was racing wildly now. I felt the urge to flee but couldn't find the strength to regain my footing.

She was hovering over me now looking into my panicked eyes with hers. How lifeless they were and as black as the darkness in which she seemed to belong. Her delicate, fragile looking hand reached down and gently embraced my throat caressing it. Fondling it.

I wanted to scream from the touch of her frozen fingers, but fear...no, *terror*...had a grip on my throat as well. Suddenly, she grabbed me with an astounding strength and lifted me up above her head still looking into my eyes, but this time I was looking down at her. I realized that my feet weren't touching the ground. How could something that seemed so weak and fragile lift a 220 pound man into the air like that? With one arm?

She smiled. It seemed the smile of a cat before pouncing on the rat that has had the misfortune of making its acquaintance. I then saw her teeth. It was the last thing I saw of her and the last time I saw her.

I don't remember much after that. Some horrifying dreams of dying and undying, but nothing more.

I found myself waking suddenly in an unknown field with the sun on the edge of the horizon. I was damn lucky to be alive, (or so I thought). At that moment I felt an uncontrollable instinct to flee or hide.

There was blood on my shirt and pain was shooting through the side of my neck. Felt like my heart was burning as well. The sun was coming up more as I laid there. That feeling of flight grew stronger. I stood up and looked around for a place to run to or hide in.

There appeared to be an old, abandoned church near a dirt road about a mile away. That struck me as odd. My vision had never been very sharp since I was a small boy. I had to wear glasses all my life and those had been lost in the attack. I knew I shouldn't be able to see that far, (especially that clearly), but that would have to be figured out later.

I began running. Running for whatever reason I could not fathom. It was pure instinct. The sun was coming. Fear was rising and, once again, was giving over to terror. The mile was covered with amazing speed. I reached the dilapidated building as the sun forced itself on the world. My skin felt like it was on fire as I entered the darkness of the church.

The cool, soothing darkness. Under the pulpit I wept and then slept.

I don't know how long I slumbered within the rotting timber and shattered windows of that haven. May have been a whole day or even days. It didn't really matter. I didn't live, (there's that word again), by days anymore. I had changed and knew I had changed. Changed in ways I would not wish upon my worst enemy.

I stayed there in that crumbling building for many months becoming more and more of what I am now. The thirst, or hunger if you wish, was incredible.

At first, I would hunt the smallest of God's creatures. Rats. Rabbits. Raccoons. Even a skunk once. Just once. With my heightened senses that one about drove me mad with the stench. Whatever came close to the building so I wouldn't have to wander too far from its shelter became my prey.

This soon became not enough. I hungered even more as time went by no matter how many of the woodland creatures I killed. Even a full grown buck that came near did not sate my appetite.

Then it happened. I still ask God for forgiveness for that moment. I did not want it to happen, but it did.

The sun had just settled in for the evening and the moon had come knocking in its fullness backlit by the stars of an autumn sky. I had awakened that dusk to the sound of something familiar. It was the sound of an ATV. It was growing stronger and stronger much like my hunger.

I crept out of my make-shift home to see what was coming. I could see the headlight weaving in and out of the sparse trees near the dirt road that lead to my sanctuary. With the time of year, I surmised it must be a hunter maybe looking for a place to set camp or perhaps a spot to set up for some night hunting.

It became clear to me, (as well as repulsive), what I must do. The hunger gripped me with a severity that I cannot describe. I followed it to its conclusion.

I stalked him...able to move as fast as his four-wheeler if not faster. I hunted the hunter. He never knew I was there. I dismounted him with one swift blow from that mechanical contraption which immediately crashed into a tree.

I slammed him into the ground and I attacked. I watched as the horror in his eyes dissolved into the coldness of lifelessness. I drank until the pulse in his veins subsided to nothing. I fed and he bled. I fed and fed and fed. The hunger was sated and I had become what I knew was inevitable. I had become...vampire.

Later that evening, after I had wept blood tears for that unknown man whose family would never know what had happened to him, (much like mine I imagined), I decided to leave that place and become part of the shadows of the rest of the world. The killing...I prefer to call it hunting, but I know what it really is...would continue, but I always made sure the target was completely dead for I did not want that person to become what I had become. I would learn to control this blood urge eventually and hunt less often over time than when I first started. I never got used to it though. That and not seeing the sun again.

I learned many things in that time between the then and now. In the shadows, I learned how much my wife and family had grieved for me. The hardest part for them seemed to have been the not knowing. Not knowing if I was actually alive or dead. How ironic...and sad...that it was both. But given time, they healed and moved on. Never forgetting, but not dwelling on it either.

I also learned more of the world than I ever imagined I could. The good and the bad. I could go into all that, but I haven't much time to do so now. The sun approaches soon.

And now, here I sit. In a funeral parlor that has been closed for hours looking at the mortal remains of the last remnant of my mortal humanity. By the way, if you are wondering, immortality isn't all it's cracked up to be. In a mortal world, you wouldn't like immortality. Everything and everyone eventually leaves you in one way or the other.

He was the only connection I had left to that world. I always watched him from afar within the shadows. I tried to keep him safe, but not too safe. After all, life isn't just to be walked through. It is to be waltzed through. He had to make his own mistakes and learn from them, but I was always there...hidden...if he needed the music to be reset. A safety net I suppose. But he didn't need it.

He did well growing up and into a man. Good in school. Lots of friends. Played sports. Went to college. Became a pediatrician and served for many years as a deacon at his church. Well-loved by the community of which he gave most of his time and energy to improving it. Had a loving wife and several children, which in turn gave him many grandchildren and great-grandchildren. I was...and am...very proud of him.

I did visit him once, but he thought I was a ghost from his past. It was on his death bed a few days ago. I visited in the night, of course, while others thought he was sleeping the sleep of fevered dreams of the slowly dying.

He called me "papaw" like he used to when he was a boy. I smiled and kissed his wrinkled forehead and told him everything was okay and that I loved him. He told me he loved me too. He quietly fell asleep. I squeezed his hand gently and then vanished back into the darkness from where I had originated.

I cried my blood tears alone that night like so many nights before, but this time not for the loss of those hunted, but for the one cherished and lost.

He died later that evening. He was 98 years of age. I look at his body now and am grateful to have known and loved him no matter how my life... *un*life... has turned out. He was the foundation of the humanity in my inhuman soul.

The dawn is coming. I have stretched out my welcome for damn close to a century and a half and now my story is up. I think it is a good day for a walk. Maybe I'll feel him holding my hand once again asking me so many questions like he did so long ago. Maybe he'll listen to the trees again as well. Yes, I think it is.

It's a good day for a walk in the sun.

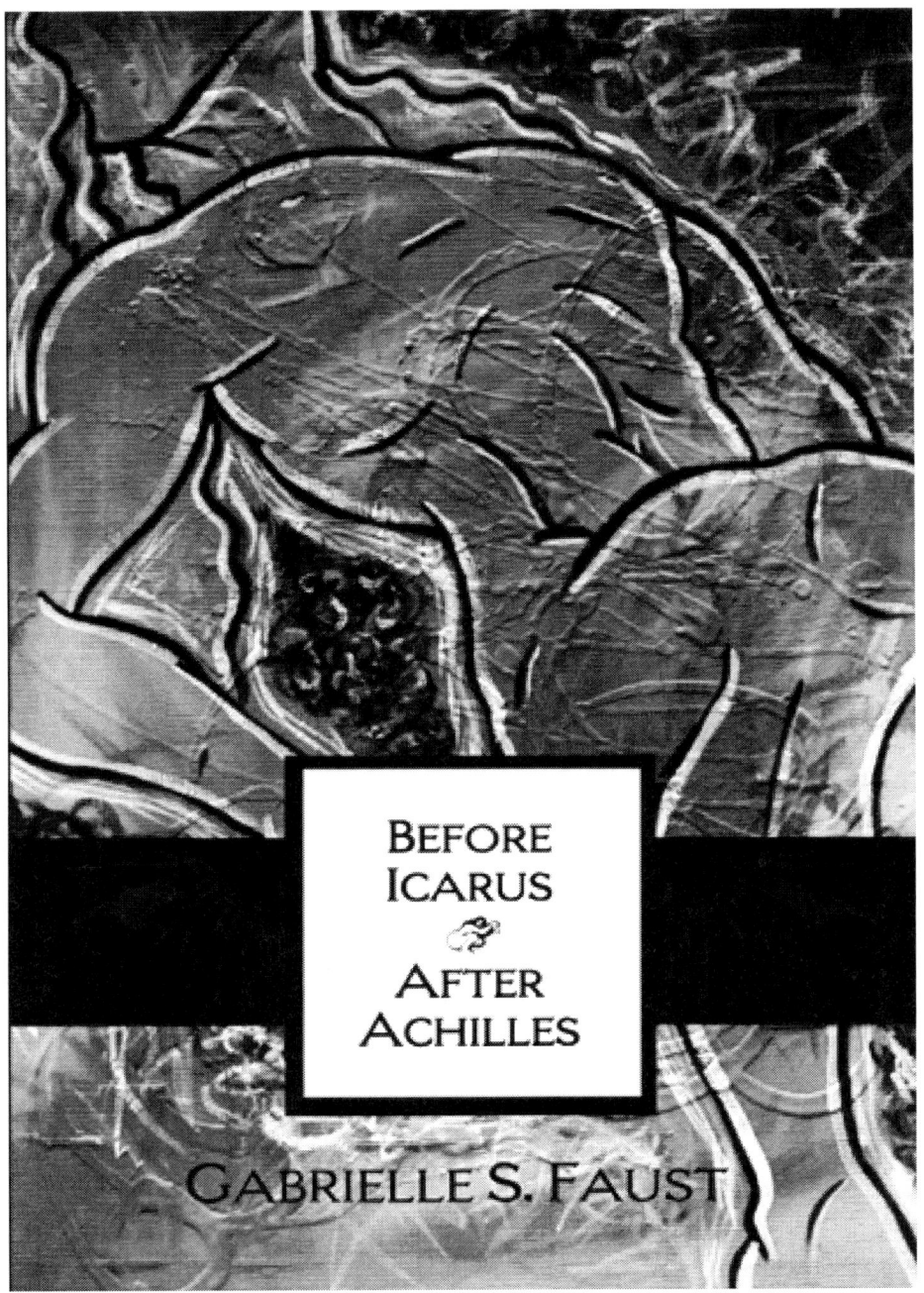

BEFORE ICARUS & AFTER ACHILLES

GABRIELLE S. FAUST

Available now at www.amazon.com and www.publishamerica.com

THE RED CLOUD AFFLICTION

By

Stanley Anderson

Alone in his classroom, Mr. Poe sat at his desk a shriveled old prune. Yet, Mr. Poe was not an elderly man. His skin was hard like scales and drawn up around his bones. The pigment had been dulled to an arid brown, for indeed, every ounce of moisture was gone from his body.

His last posture, relaxed in his chair, was forever engraved in his tendons and bones. His head was slanted to the side in a final surrender of energy. His mouth hung in a frozen cry of woe. His brow was creased in the middle unveiling the indisputable hurt in his cold and soulless eyes.

Still, his message would go unnoticed by the room of empty desks before him. Beyond these was a row of windows running from one side of the room to the other, giving him a glimpse of some evolving world before he was given to darkness. Behind him sat the tables that satisfied his students' curiosity. Within the drawers were utensils of chrome, metal, and iron that aided their exploration. Sinks sat along the wall to cleanse their hands of stains wrought from their debasing duties.

Situated away from everything else was a closet.

And for a time, all this was shrouded in a profound silence.

Then, Joey entered the room. Always the first arrival, the good student, the one with promise, his practiced greeting for his mentor was hushed by surprise. The instructor wasn't ready to receive it.

Not expecting Mr. Poe's uncharitable disposition, Joey paused. He knew Mr. Poe to be a stern man, but he was not so elite that he would ignore someone. And Mr. Poe was never still, claiming idleness made him fidgety. But now he was very still. Joey examined further.

With each step, Joey learned more. When he confronted the specimen that Mr. Poe represented, a natural desire to flee rushed to the surface of Joey's skin and straightened every hair on his body. When faced with the grotesque world of biology, many of his fellow students would dare venture no further. But he was the good student. Remembering Mr. Poe's advice, he examined closer.

Joey never thought this day would come, but it was clear Mr. Poe was dead. Yet, Mr. Poe always taught him that there was an explanation to everything. Joey searched, but his initial attempt was limited to Mr. Poe's body alone, and thus, he learned little. But he remembered what Mr. Poe said when something like this happened: broaden your search.

Lying in front of Mr. Poe was a note. A pen lay on this note, the point indicating the last word that was written. Joey picked up the note and read it:

I apologize to the one who finds me in this state, but no time must be spent on fruitless grieving or speculation. If anything, the departed should be respected and it is in this regard that I write my last wish. I admit my peers would label this a strange favor, but the influence of death does invoke unusual responses from everyone involved. Therefore, I ask, without reserve, that I be placed in the space cast aside from all that makes up this room.

Joey glanced away from the note, looked past the corpse, and targeted the lone closet on the other side. Indeed, this was a strange request. But he knew Mr. Poe to be a strange man. Fellow students claimed that Mr. Poe never left his classroom. They said he even slept here. Why he did this, they didn't know, but Joey wanted to find out. One night he crept back onto campus to observe Mr. Poe's building. As if the rumors were true, Mr. Poe's classroom was the only one with lights on. Curious, Joey crept closer. He stopped whenever he saw Mr. Poe's shadow dance along one of the walls inside. He saw this through the windows on the side where all the lab tables were.

Maybe Mr. Poe had a late night preparing for tomorrow and was just now packing up. However, Joey had waited an hour and still, Mr. Poe remained inside the classroom. Determined to see that Mr. Poe hadn't slept in his own classroom, Joey decided to wait, but to his dismay, all the lights went off inside the building. Mr. Poe never came out.

Still, Joey waited. He would wait all night if he had to. Mr. Poe himself taught him how to be a patient researcher.

When his patience almost reached its limit, Joey saw something. It wasn't Mr. Poe. It was someone else. They were heading toward Mr. Poe's classroom. From what Joey could tell, this was a homeless person: dressed in rags, long untidy hair, and a brown sack in his hand. Probably a beer. The bum stumbled toward the front door to Mr. Poe's building. There was purpose in the bum's direction. Maybe he had a meeting with Mr. Poe. Yet, a meeting this late at night, and a meeting with a bum both seemed peculiar.

However, the bum reached Mr. Poe's door. To Joey's surprise, the door was unlocked. The bum went in closing the door behind him. None of the lights came on due to the bum's visit. As a matter of fact, nothing happened for a couple of minutes. Then, Joey saw the faint glow from within through those same windows. The glow lasted a few seconds and after that, Joey saw or heard nothing else for the rest of the time he remained there.

The next day, he wanted to confront Mr. Poe about the bum's visit but instead marveled at how cheery Mr. Poe seemed that day.

Mr. Poe gave no goodbyes in his note, but one bit of information was scribbled at the bottom. What Joey felt in those last desperate words was that Mr. Poe was betrayed. Studying Mr. Poe's expression again, Joey glanced at the desk remembering the pen. He didn't notice this before, but now he saw the blood on the pen's sides. He picked it up to look closer. The blood was fashioned onto the pen's surface is precise patterns. They were finger prints.

Joey carefully picked Mr. Poe's hands up. His wrists were stubborn against Joey's insistence, but Joey was able to see his fingertips. Like the rest of his body, Mr. Poe's fingers were dry. Joey could've used the element of time as a way of explaining that the blood was Mr. Poe's, but the blood was fresh. Mr. Poe appeared to be in this state for a long time.

Examining the bloody fingerprints brought a chilling memory to mind. He had seen fingerprints like these before. There were several instances he could recall, while in Mr. Poe's classroom, hearing someone say something just behind him, a voice he didn't recognize. Not understanding what they said, he would turn to find no one was there. Yet, he remembered feeling their hand on his shoulder when they spoke. Looking at his shoulder, he saw bloody finger prints on his shirt.

Did one of his classmates hurt themselves and need help? When he looked around, everyone was getting along with their studies just fine.

In other instances like this, he not only had the same finger prints on his shoulder, but would find his pencil or notebook missing when it was right in front of him before. He would discover his lost item somewhere on the floor nearby, and they would always have bloody finger prints on them.

Maybe someone was playing a trick on him, or maybe…it was something else. Yet, he couldn't say that he was in danger, because during one of these instances, he was taking a test and broke the lead of his pencil. Instead of having to get up during the silence and sharpen his pencil, another one appeared on his desk…with those same bloody finger prints.

Maybe it was a game, but the game went too far this time. Whoever it was had tricked Mr. Poe. But *he* would not betray his mentor. Once again, and undoubtedly the last, Joey took Mr. Poe's instructions. Looking past the corpse, Joey targeted the lone closet and knew that was where Mr. Poe wanted to be. Indeed, he felt it strange, but who was he to argue?

Carefully, respectfully, he carried Mr. Poe to the closet. Once opened, the closet resembled a coffin. Joey saw that was meaning behind this strange request. Now that Mr. Poe's bent corpse was propped up inside this coffin-like closet, Joey said goodbye and closed the door.

The door had a small window near the top. Joey looked into its darkness. A light flicked on from within and Joey was given one last glimpse of Mr. Poe.

Yet, Joey gained more than just a look. A new sound accompanied the light from the fixture inside the closet. Joey could only relate this sound to the gradual escalation of a machine hum. But as to the cause of this sudden awakening, Joey didn't know. Could it have been something within the intricacies of Mr. Poe's last wish? If so, then Joey was feeling accomplished. Because he responded without question, perhaps he would be rewarded. Ah yes, the note was just the initiative. Mr. Poe had it all planned out and the one who granted him his last wish would go unscathed. All evidence would be wiped away and no questions would fall upon the honorable volunteer.

Joey was curious about one thing, however: how would the evidence be wiped clean?

Joey flinched and a swift blur caught his eye. It was a red blur, he remembered. His attention fell upon his right arm. To his horror, blood covered the top side of his forearm. He recalled his previous flinch resulted from a strange sensation. Could he have been struck by something, or worse, bitten? But why bitten? There were no marks on his skin. Only the presence of blood. Was it even his blood? He glanced at the wall. There, beside the closet door, was another spat of blood. Streams dripped from the mass down the wall. None of this was here a few seconds ago, but before Joey could even begin to speculate, the red blur skipped from his forearm and splattered against the wall again. He experienced that same sensation as before. It felt like a suction. And the blood on the wall, that was his. Again, a cloud of his blood leaped from his forearm and splattered against the wall. This time, Joey heard something that troubled him more than watching his own blood leave his body. He heard a voice accompany this occurrence. From the time his blood escaped his arm and splattered against the wall, he heard a single syllable uttered like " aht!" And it was a man's voice. But it wasn't Mr. Poe.

The red cloud passed again with the sound, "aht!" and Joey felt himself tingling all over now. His conscious told him this wasn't a good sign. His own blood was being sucked from his body. However, after studying this strange sucking sensation and his tingling body, he realized he felt no pain. More accurately, it felt like a pleasant release.

He equated his reaction to a drug induction. And because he allotted this sensation with his reward, karma silenced the hum of the machine. The red cloud didn't pass yet the light inside the closet remained on.

Joey was enraptured as he watched his blood erase from the wall as though it were being taken inside the building itself. But why? He looked into the window of the closet.

A tear formed at the corner of both Mr. Poe's dried eye lids. The tears rushed along the bottom lids and then spread across the whites of his eyes. When this moisture reached his pupils, Mr. Poe blinked. The moisture was amplified by this natural means of preservation, and Mr. Poe regained the use of his eyes. The amount of moisture was slight, thus his movements were limited. Yet, he had enough to realize where he was.

"I'm....awake." he willed himself to say, but only his mind spoke his words. He looked through the window into the classroom. Joey was looking back at him. They both shared the same shock.

"Joey…" Mr. Poe's mind spoke again, but Joey didn't get the message.

The amount of moisture reached its limit and Mr. Poe lost his abilities. Yet, somehow, he was granted the right to continue seeing.

"He woke up!" Joey whispered. His excitement had stolen his breath. He pressed his face against the window and beat against the door.

"Mr. Poe! Mr. Poe!" he found his voice again, though he received no answer. Once more, Mr. Poe took on the resemblance of a mere specimen. But Joey knew that for a moment, Mr. Poe had come back to life. He looked at his bloody arm. He looked at the wall. He remembered the machine hum. He grinned. The reward was different than he first envisioned. In fact, it was greater. He would help bring Mr. Poe back to life.

Just as he reached this conclusion, the machine started up again. The red cloud that was his blood leaped from his arm and splattered against the same spot on the wall. He heard that voice again: "aht!"

Then he heard more voices. These voices emanated from elsewhere. They were the voices of his classmates. He gasped turning a worried look toward the door to the classroom. A few minutes and class would start. The other students were showing up right on time.

"Aht!" The red cloud jumped again.

What would his classmates think if they saw what was happening? Their misunderstanding would leave Mr. Poe asleep, throw questions upon questions at Joey, and ultimately deprive him of his reward. They didn't know the story.

"Aht!" the red cloud jumped.

Time was not on his side. The intervals between the red clouds' jump was too long, and he knew each amount taken from him was only so much given to Mr. Poe. That's why Mr. Poe only came to life for that brief.....

Joey now realized his thinking was self-centered. He counted only himself in light of Mr. Poe's awakening, but common sense dictated he was not enough. Should he bring Mr. Poe back, it would cost him his life, and honorable Mr. Poe would have no such thing. If more people were involved, then the chances of people dying from sacrificing more than they could would be less. It was brilliant.

"Aht!" the cloud said.

Joey frowned considering the nature of the process. He was a brave student taught to venture further if anything was to be learned. However, he couldn't say the same for his fellow students. Splitting open a frog was enough to test the limits of some, but watching their own blood go airborne felt worlds beyond dismantling a mere dead animal.

"Aht!" the cloud jumped and he smirked at the tingling in his body. The nature of that sensation captured his thoughts, and he considered other possibilities. He remembered describing this suction as a pleasant release. He remembered his initial fear was calmed by this pleasantness. He let his smirk stretch into a smile. His smile turned into a chuckle. Whether his idea gave him this joy or the release influenced this joy from him, he now concluded his classmates would react just the same.

He looked into the closet window and smiled at Mr. Poe.

"I understand now." he said, "but I need you to wait. I won't be enough. Let the others come in. There will be more to take from if you wait until then."

There was a click and the hum of the machine wound down to a sigh.

"Thank you!" he squealed and ran off to the restroom to wash his arm.

The blood on the wall was taken into the structure and Mr. Poe was given his voice.

"Joey." he whispered, his voice raspy from its previous drought.

"Joey!" he pushed, but his voice couldn't reach beyond the closet door.

More blood was taken in this instance, yet his time was limited just as before. He lost what voice he had and was forced to watch through the window.

The hour chimed and the students entered the classroom. The walls remained silent as the rows of desks were filled with bodies and lots of chatter. None noticed the glowing window of the closet door.

Several minutes went by before Joey stepped out of the restroom beside the lab tables. Prior his appearance, few students drew away from their conversations to notice Mr. Poe's absence. When Joey appeared, they asked him about Mr. Poe's whereabouts.

"Oh, Mr. Poe went out for a minute." Joey offered, "He'll be back shortly."

Joey took his seat which was situated near the lone closet. He sat next to a circle of friends. The most outspoken of them was a guy named Reggie. Even now, Reggie played his social role as smooth as he always had, reaching out to the girl of the group with hands that mimicked claws and making a sound that resembled a hiss. The girl, Laura, just waved him off saying, "Oh, whatever, you enjoy that class too much."

The class she spoke of, Joey understood from previous conversations, was World Literature. Today's subject was....

"I'll wrap my lips around your neck and suck you dry," Reggie warned her. Two girls outside their circle giggled at his approach to courtship.

"You've got to have the fangs to do it," Laura shot back. "And besides, it's daytime. Better go back to your cemetery before you burn."

Vampires. Joey knew the subject was of myth and legend, yet he couldn't help but relate it to Mr. Poe's situation.

"No, no, honey," Reggie corrected, "All I have to do is bite. You won't care after that."

Laura wore a coy smirk, "Don't flatter yourself."

Joey felt that the tingling sensation he experienced when his blood was drained was much like a Vampire's tantalizing bite. Even if this was a quixotic perspective on Mr. Poe's situation, he threw caution to the wind and knew everything would be alright.

"Okay, Mr. Poe," he whispered to the closet, "it's okay to start now."

No one noticed the waking hum of the machine. Joey knew the moment of truth was mere seconds away. A girl sitting in the back off the room jumped when someone told her "aht!" and a red cloud passed between her and the wall. The student adjacent from her noticed this occurrence. After sharing curious glances, they noticed the blood on the wall. It was the adjacent student who then noticed the blood that covered the back of the girl's shirt.

"Aht!" another red cloud fell to the floor. A student's bare leg was covered in blood.

"What happened?" a witness asked, but the afflicted student had no explanation.

"Aht!" the occurrence happened elsewhere. Blood covered a leg of the person's desk and splattered on the floor.

"Did you see that?" another witness gasped. The afflicted student lifted his bloody palm to examine it in shock. Then he, along with those around him, watched as his blood bubbled to the surface and then washed around to the back of his hand to fall onto the leg of his desk. They all heard the "aht!" sound that accompanied this occurrence.

One boy leaped from his seat. A red cloud jumped from his stomach and skipped across the top of his desk splattering the student in front of him. He took a couple of steps back, but a red cloud jumped from his bloody stomach again. In a panic, he brushed at the blood on his shirt soaking his palms, but this didn't prevent another cloud from jumping onto his desk again.

"It's blood!" a girl gasped, and the whole class now understood.

"Blood!" another gasped.

"Blood," another repeated.

"Blood?" another asked.

When the announcement was passed around, the students started to giggle.

"Blood," they snickered.

"It's blood," they started to chuckle.

The more this occurrence spread, the more everyone joined in to laugh, and the "aht!" voices sped up. Now, all the students were afflicted.

Reggie was giggling at the sight of several students pointing at the windows in the back of the room. Many red clouds were leaping from their bodies and splattering onto the glass at different intervals. Though, the whole space between them and the windows was cluttered with a ceaseless cloud of blood. To Reggie, it looked like horizontal rain.

He looked past Laura whose shoulder gave blood to the backrest of her seat. There was another girl sitting in the next row over. She was laughing to the point of tears as her face was nothing but a red mask of her own blood. Whenever the red cloud jumped from her face and splattered on the floor, Reggie lost sight of her eyes, but could still see her gaping mouth, her blood stretching from her lips in thick tendrils.

Despite his own amusement at a red cloud leaping from his chest onto his desk, the sight of that girl's face stole the excitement from him. His laughter dulled to a quiet chuckle, and he looked ahead at Joey. While everyone else was laughing, Joey was the only one who kept his cool. In fact, he seemed to understand what was happening. Joey had his right arm extended and watched as the red cloud jumped from his forearm to splatter against the wall beside the closet.

Reggie leaned forward trying to fight against the tingling sensation, "Hey, Joey, what's going on?"

Joey turned around and Reggie could see his classmate's mind was elsewhere.

"It's for Mr. Poe. Can't you see? We're all going to bring him back to life. Everyone only has to sacrifice a little bit. Don't worry."

Reggie didn't understand what Joey was talking about, but as he looked at all the blood covering the floor, the desks, the windows, even some parts of the ceiling, this looked more like a slaughter house than some generous donation, yet everyone was blinded by their own amusement to even notice.

"Joey," he said, "meet me outside…at the park…near the big tree. Can you do that?"

Joey's tranquil smile faltered, "Uh, okay."

Reggie forced himself to his feet. There was no way he could stop what was happening. All he knew was that everyone needed to get out of here. He grabbed the giggling Laura by the wrist and dragged her toward the door.

"Adam! Spence!" he called to his other giggling friends, "Come on. I've got something to show you."

Still giggling, Adam and Spence got up from their seats. If Reggie had something to further entertain them, then they would follow.

Now that Reggie had moved away from his desk, the red cloud jumped from his chest and splattered onto the floor. After every couple of steps his blood made a new splatter in front of him. Even if he felt weak, he wouldn't stop. He knew stopping would only result in death. Yet, someone clasped him on his shoulder with a strong grip. Feeling the strain on his body, he turned to his right to see who prevented him from leaving. But when he looked, there was no one there. The grip had lifted just as soon as he turned to look. Had he imagined it? Then he saw the evidence that proved someone had grabbed him. There was a perfect shape of a hand print on his shoulder. The print was made with blood.

"Aaaahhhhwaaaanttt!" he heard someone groan from his left. He felt the grip on his left shoulder and when he turned, he saw a smile. It was a quick smile. A bloody smile from someone he didn't know. There was no way he could've known, because this person's skin had been stripped away revealing everything underneath. That lipless smile was induced because nothing was there to inhibit it. And those eyes had targeted him, the muscles of the brow contracting to create a scowl.

Reggie flinched just by the sheer shock of seeing this skinless person, and that had been what removed the grip on his shoulder and made the person disappear. Now, only Laura was at his side still laughing and giving blood to the floor. If he had seen something, then that only made the situation worse. But he couldn't decide whether that skinless person had stood beside him just now or not. The trauma he was feeling now was real enough.

He turned to the students, "Everyone! Something bad is happening!"

Regardless their amusement, the students heard Reggie's warning.

"We need to go outside! Hurry!" He told them. No longer able to stand the tingling in his body, he pushed open the door and stumbled out. Inside, maybe it was some sort of morbid curiosity, but some of the students followed Reggie's insistence. However, many of them were too deeply afflicted to notice his verbal warning.

As if a switch went off in their heads, Reggie and his friends became sober to the affliction. Being outside the building seemed safe, yet they stood an extra distance away. Those who followed them out sat down a few feet from the building due to exhaustion. They were still giggling, and Reggie saw why. The building was still taking their blood into the outside walls.

He and his friends added more distance between them and the building.

"Hey!" one of the afflicted called, "Come out! You've got to see this!"

Reggie's eyes sparkled with hope. He remembered having little confidence in his announcement to the class, but it was all he could manage then. More students did come out, but, they stood next to the building and watched the red clouds start to jump from their bodies.

"You've got to be kidding me." Reggie groaned.

"Get away from there!" Laura cried to those afflicted students.

Reggie instantly thought of Joey. If only they could get him outside.

He cupped his hands around his mouth and called, "Joey! Joey!"

Adam and Spence helped him, "Joey! Joey, where are you?"

"Hahaa! Joey!" one of the inflicted students shouted. "Joey! Joey!"

Reggie and his friends stopped when the rest of the inflicted students picked up the cry. They were laughing the whole time, seeming to be cheering for Joey rather than calling for him.

As this went on, Joey finally appeared in one of the windows along the wall where the lab tables stood inside. He was covered in splotches of blood.

"Hey! There he is!" one student cheered and the other students took up the cheer and clapped their hands.

"Heeey!" he called back.

"Joey!" Reggie shouted drawing Joey's attention. "Come outside! We need to talk to you!" Yet the moment he spoke those words, he knew it was futile. Joey's eyes were looking through Reggie, gazing at the space beyond.

"I'm sorry." Joey responded, "but I'm about to turn things up. Get away if you're not helping."

"Wait! Joey!" Reggie gasped, but Joey disappeared. Reggie started toward the building, but Laura stopped him.

"You feel that?" she asked.

He didn't at first, but then he felt the sudden gust of wind. Within the wind, he felt that unnatural suction he experienced when the red clouds jumped.

"Look!" Spence gasped.

All around them, loose objects were being swept up by this wind. The suction intensified causing trees to bend toward the building. The students sitting outside rolled about and laughed as the red clouds jumped in accelerated intervals. Their whole bodies were faucets now. The red clouds resembled their shapes from head to toe and splattered their silhouettes onto the outside walls.

"It's no good!" Adam shouted pulling on Laura and Spence. Laura grabbed Reggie and they all ran for the park. The wind fought against their escape, and they knew it was trying to take them along with the other students. So they persisted. Because they persisted, so did the wind. They screamed when parts of their skin tried to pull away. Reggie slapped his hand over his left eyebrow to hold that part of his face down. Regardless of their awareness of the situation, the intensified suction caused them to giggle as they ran.

Inside, the students were no longer laughing. They were no longer alive. Their bodies were thrown about like rag dolls as parts and blood were stripped away and pasted to the building's interior.

Joey had his face plastered against the window of Mr. Poe's closet.

"It won't be long," he managed to say just before his head was taken apart piece by piece.

When there was nothing left to take, the hum of the machine slowed to a sigh. The interior of the building was cleansed by the absorption of all the blood and body parts. The light inside the closet snapped off and the door unlatched.

Mr. Poe stepped out looking well for a man of fifty-two, but his face was drawn with a deep frown. He was all alone in his classroom again. He looked up at the ceiling in defiance.

"Are you satisfied?" he scoffed.

The voice sounded one last time, "aht!" and a gush of blood jumped from Mr. Poe to the ceiling. Mr. Poe was left as the shriveled up corpse Joey found him as before.

Satisfied, the building shifted beyond its structured capabilities. The walls curved and swelled with a thumping pulse. The short and multi-toned "aht!" was transformed into a long and variant moan.

From the park, Reggie and his friends watched the building come to life.

"Well, now what do we do?" Adam asked.

Still mesmerized by what he saw, Reggie just shrugged, "I bet it has a heart."

JUST A GIRL
By
Andrea Colleen

As the only girl in an all male crew, I had to prove myself plenty of times. I always had to be on my guard and hold my own no matter what, but it was never a problem. In 1929, women may have just been starting to make tentative forays out of the kitchen and into the man's world, but I had already elbowed my way right into the den, grabbed a scotch, and made myself nice and comfortable. Many of the men called me intense, and most of them also called me a bitch behind my back - what they didn't understand was that I relished that title; strove to be the biggest bitch that I could be. It may not have earned me a lot of friends, but it earned me respect, without a doubt. A broad had to be a tough bitch to be even a soldier in the outfit, let alone the hatchet girl that I was

The Italians had been steadily encroaching on our territory for the past six months. Loading up the speakeasies with booze cheaper than ours while at the same time paying off the cops and politicians more, selling their dirty whores at discount prices, and just plain undercutting our businesses at every turn. But they had finally done the big deed in killing an up and coming member of our crew and pissed off my Boss. And he meant to show them, and the other generals, that he was not to be fucked with. Stepping on the toes of the nastiest motherfucker this side of, well... anywhere, was not to be advised, and they'd gone and done it. Frankie was mad about it, too - not just mad but infuriated and very personally offended, and he planned to do something about it. Something drastic.

"Those fucking cunts!" he raged at me over the phone. "They're gonna get theirs - oh, yes... they are." He huffed heavily for a second then continued. "You get yer pretty arse over here and you do it quick, Billie-girl," he growled. "An' bring yer kit." I smiled as I heard the phone slam down in my ear, laying the receiver in the cradle as I kicked off my heels and began removing my stockings.

I arrived in the alley behind the clubhouse twenty minutes later dressed in black and in men's clothing - straight leg fitted pin stripe trousers, black dress shirt, even a matching vest and wide tie. Women's clothes were better for hiding weapons, but men's were better for quantity and they allowed more ease of movement in... tense situations. I pulled my black case from where it was stashed in the trunk, running my fingers briefly over the ornate silver initialing before I made my way in through the service entrance, finding Frankie in his private office with 'Sad Charlie' McDougan and Seamus 'Mick' Irish.

"Hey, Red," Mick nodded to me when I entered, and I patted his shoulder as I passed him on my way to the desk. Now I knew we were really going to go all the way - Frankie had gathered up the serious movers for his crew this run. I smiled at Charlie as I walked by and he reached up and tipped his fedora slightly, winking at me before I met Frankie's eyes.

"Billie-girllll....." he purred, reaching out his meaty hands while grinning that shark bite grin at me; that sharp-toothed split in his face that made me want to curl up into a little ball and rock back and forth. Everyone was scared of Frankie and that grin, me included, but it was the times he directed it at me that I was glad I had never followed in the footsteps of my whoring mother. At least I didn't ever have to see that grin coming at me in bed. He took my hand and guided me around the desk, patting his thigh, insinuating that I should sit on his lap as he grinned at me; feral and cold. I smiled back sweetly even though inside I was cringing and perched myself gingerly on his knee. He motioned for the other two men to sit in the chairs facing the desk and then laid out the plan.

"Alright, men," he chuckled briefly while patting me on the ass before he got down to business. "Here's wot it is: these bastard Dago's been stickin' their grimy fingers into every little pie we've got, an' I'm done with it. All the basics been covered - one of their own gave 'em up, the stupid fuck. He tol' me who's there and how to get in and then I turned off his light for 'im, so no one knows we're comin'. We're not playin' here, kids - we come fast an' heavy -I want 'em all done, an' done up right." His heavy paw squeezed tightly on the arm of the chair and then released slowly, a sure sign that he was getting excited. So was I.

He got up and headed for the door, all three of us in a silent line behind him through the corridors. We got into the back of an empty delivery van in the alley, and Frankie shut the doors then pounded on the metal partition between us and the cab before the engine rumbled to life. It was hot as hell in there, made even more stifling by the fact that I was stuffed into a little box with three big, scary fuckers, shoulder to shoulder and on our way to a bloodbath. Frankie was crushed up close next to me and Mick and Charlie were pressed in tight on the opposite bench. You could almost savor the excitement in the air, each man checking his weapons, the clicking of metal the only sound in the hollow space.

My hands were starting to shake just a little as I opened the gear kit between my legs, lovingly fondling my hammer before I slid it into one of my belt loops. The hammer's my favorite, but only for the up close and personal work; persuasions, if you will. Then I pulled my knife from its sheath and slid its razor edge back and forth along the stone a few more times, just to make sure it was as sharp as could be. That, I tucked into my right boot in the specially made hidden 'pocket' there - just in case. My back up was next, the smallest Tommy gun produced - I clicked the pieces together, loaded it, and strapped it across my back before stroking the barrel a few times as I smiled. I was in my own little world, happily preparing to commit murder, and thinking simply 'fuck, I love my job.'

Finally I pulled out my piece - a sleek silver weapon of destruction - my baby, my iron fist. But most importantly, my equalizer. A bullet fired from my Colt could take down the biggest of men, therefore making a moot point of the battle of the sexes. Still smiling, I rubbed the soft cloth over the silver finish, making it shine, then kissing the barrel. When I looked up, all three of my companions were watching me and grinning.

"You're a strange bird, Billie-girl." Frank chuckled, slinging his arm around my shoulders and squeezing. "Never met a bird who liked killin' so damn much..."

"I never met one who liked it at all - 'cept you, Red." Charlie said softly.

"What can I say, it's a gift." I responded with a shining smile.

The truck rumbled forward, swaying slightly, and as I rocked along with it I thought about why I did like to kill so much. I was sure that if my father had come back from the war and my mother hadn't been forced to become a prostitute, I would have turned out a lot different. There were other events, of course, that led me to where I was, but that had been the source. What had that nurse in the institution called me after my last arrest? Sociopath? That sounded about right. Then the van turned, tires crunching on gravel before we coasted to a stop. Frankie's voice was a dangerous whisper.

"Alright now, here's the specs. Warehouse. Big and mostly empty. Unlocked fire door in the back, we'll sneak right in. That's right by the office, which is where all those fuckers are. When we round the corner, there will be a big window between the warehouse and the office - when you see that you let fly. Keep shooting until there ain't nothin' moving in that office, you understand?" All three of us nodded, hands on our weapons. That was it - just the way it should be. That was the premier crew, the best of the best, everything had been set up for us and now we were there; primed and ready to obliterate.

My adrenalin crept up one more level and my palms started to sweat. I wiped them, one at a time, on my trousers as I waited for

Frankie to open the door. It looked to me like the others were itching as hard as I was to get the show on the road. He swung the door wide and helped me out, leading me around to the front as the other two stepped out and closed up the van. They always sent me in first - it was a crucial element of surprise for our crew, no gangster ever expected his death to come from a woman.

I flexed my fingers and stretched my back like a cat, silently creeping across the cool cement of the loading dock towards the tiny door on the side. My heart was pounding so hard I all I could hear was the rush of blood in my head, my nipples rock hard against the rough fabric of the men's shirt. The door pushed easily open, not a sound from it or any of us as we filed inside, Frankie so close up behind me that I could feel the heat coming off of him in waves. Charlie was next and Mick was bringing up the rear, all of our weapons gleaming in the dull light. Around a few crates and I could see the light shining from the office window, and I felt that familiar tingling coming over me. One hand gripped tight on my Colt and the other absently stroked the handle of the hammer as we inched closer and closer.

The corner loomed ahead and I knew that just around it I would get to be the right hand of death, its sweet destruction. The throbbing wetness between my legs was not unexpected - I was on fire, so ready; if only I could kill and then fuck, it would be perfect. I couldn't creep anymore, I was too close, the kill was too close, and it was all always over far too fast. I slid around the corner, my gun held loosely in my outstretched arms, my eyes sharp slits scanning the empty office. Empty - what the fuck?!?

Frankie came right up behind me, Tommy gun in each hand, arms spread around either side of me, only to freeze like I was. The other two followed slowly, eyeing the quizzical looks on our faces. We all stared into the bare space, lights blazing but nothing else looking out of the ordinary. Except that there was nobody there and there was supposed to be seven guys waiting for us to end their miserable lives.

"We've been set up." Frankie growled quietly. It vibrated off my spine and sent shivers through me. I was going to die that night.

With every hair on my body standing straight up, I started moving back the way we had come in. As I crept towards the corner, I scanned the warehouse for our would-be victims, but could see nothing in the deep, murky shadows. Frankie's bulky frame was moving in a surprisingly agile manner as he made his way towards me, with Mick and Charlie backing up just behind him, their rifles trained outward into the dark. We moved as one stealthy machine for several long, tense seconds where I thought that maybe, just maybe, we were wrong and it was all a lark.

Just as I was about to slip back around the corner, a gun shot rang out and a burning bullet screamed into my right shoulder, slamming me back against the wall, which I promptly slid down. My head throbbed and so did my shoulder, blood slicking down my arm and torso. I thought I heard Frankie's voice shout my name, but it sounded far away. Opening my eyes I saw Charlie's long legs begin to dart past where I was slumped, but several shots put him on the concrete near my feet. His numerous wounds caused the blood to pool so quickly around him that he turned gray right there in front of my blurry eyes, seeming even paler by the sea of crimson surrounding him. Usually blood didn't bother me, but I felt nauseous. Perhaps it was that I was losing so much of my own.

I closed my eyes and heard quick footsteps echoing through the warehouse, coming closer. I could hear Frankie desperately whispering to Mick, and the stocky man grunting in reply. I kept trying to press the heel of my hand against the weeping wound in my shoulder, but I just didn't have the strength to keep the pressure on or even hold my arm up. Tommy guns... I listened to Frankie firing wildly into the darkness, the war cry of a dead man howling from his throat. He stopped and I listened to the echoes chase each other around the mammoth cavern for several seconds before an answering round of gunfire lit up the room. Mick was down before he even cocked that sawed-off of his, the bullets pummeling his body and making it jerk like a puppet.

Soon after that Frankie's harsh panting was in my right ear; he was next to me on the wall, wounded as I was. He was cursing under his breath and trying to wriggle his revolver out of its holster with his non-dominant hand. Heavy footsteps came right up to us and I cracked my eyes open. Yep, we were set up.

"You wanted Mannagge, you fucking cunt - you got it," the Don's grating voice ground out. I was really starting to fade in and out of consciousness at that point, and wishing to stay out because I knew these Italians weren't going to leave until our whole crew was done. I heard several shots boom in quick succession, so close that I was sure they were meant for me, until I felt Frankie's weight crushing into my side. Then it was gone and I heard his dead body smack wetly against the floor several feet away from me.

I felt hands pulling at me, not picking me up but... loosening my clothes, I thought. It could be the paramedics, I hoped feverishly. I forced my eyes to open, first seeing my weapons scattered around me on the floor. Then I noticed that my vest and shirt were ripped open and that my trousers and panties were pulled down to my knees, exposing the bare skin underneath. I had a second to wonder what the hell was going on before I started to fade again. Someone slapped my cheek.

"Hey... hey!" Another slap. I cracked my eyes open, but it was so damn hard. "Pay attention, Don Gilionie has something to say to you." I look up at the older man who was staring at my naked body.

"I'm not gonna kill you because you are just a girl," he said in that thick accent, still not looking at my face. For the first time in my life I kept my mouth shut and did not respond to that statement. I simply closed my eyes again.

I listened to the retreating footsteps of the Don and his crew, unable to move as I was very rapidly going into shock. I decided I really didn't care anymore if I lived or died. They would probably lock me in that women's 'institution' for life now. I heard sirens in the distance as that fuzzy, black feeling flowed up the back of my neck and my mind went blank...

2007 ANNUAL COMPILATION

WORD WEAVERS

Available now at www.lulu.com

THE SLIDING

By

Kevin Lucia

November, 2007

I've broken a promise made long ago; and I don't know what's going to happen.

The cursor on my *Imac* blinks, daring me to continue what I'd started months ago. What once seemed safe now feels foolish. I'm dancing at the edge of something terrible, but I don't know if I can stop, or want to, for that matter.

Maybe it's the long nights, which have only become more desolate since Jennifer packed her bags and left, or the cold bed I wake up in every morning. Maybe it's driving to work and eating alone; or maybe it's the dead eyes looking back at me from the mirror, dull and flat with emptiness.

I called Joel and Chris the other day, but the conversation fizzled. They remember three high school kids trespassing in an old house, nothing more. Even with the gentlest prodding, I couldn't get their shuttered memories past a certain point. To them, nothing important happened.

However; something important *did* happen. One August Saturday afternoon we glimpsed a dark, powerful truth: that a shadowed world exists next to ours, one that defies explanation.

Slowly, my fingers engage the keys, initially hesitant, but with each keystroke the corridors in my mind widen. With care, I again open doors shut long ago, wondering if tonight the things sliding in the dark would claim me at last.

***

August, 1988

I hesitated on the old porch outside the closed window, hand resting lightly on cracked siding. Through dirty glass the room appeared empty, littered with the debris you'd expect in an abandoned house.

"This's stupid," I breathed, scanning the window, wondering if it'd shatter when opened. "You seriously want to do this?"

I couldn't see but heard the smirk in Joel's voice. "C'mon; you're the biggest guy here. Don't tell me you're chicken."

I glared at him over my shoulder. Joel and I'd been friends since kindergarten, but sometimes he pissed me off. I'm cautious by nature and he's not, especially when *I'm* going first.

"Listen, *you* may not have football this fall, but I do. I don't want to miss the season because I sliced myself on a broken window messing around."

"Honestly, Joel," Chris said, leaning against the siding, "that window wasn't closed up last summer. Maybe this isn't smart."

Chris's support strengthened me. "Okay, we can open this — I'm just gonna need a hand, because the frame's weak, and I don't want the glass to break." I grasped one corner of the window, and nodded at the other. "Chris…?"

He nodded; moving quickly, without second thought.

As we carefully tried to open the window, I asked, "So what's the deal with this place?"

The story was typical. Bassler House was an old, three story Victorian house that had stood abandoned for years, and every summer when Chris and his brother visited their grandmother at Clifton Lake, they took a pilgrimage here to test their mettle. According to Chris, its walls and floors were adorned with hastily scrawled Satan-worshiping paraphernalia: pentagrams, 666 and predictable slogans such as *"Satan Rulz"* and *"Jesus Suks"*.

"It's lame," Chris finished as the window opened, "it was fun to poke around as kids, but there's not much here."

"That's only because we haven't gone into the basement yet," Joel added from behind us.

I glanced downward at the crumbling foundation and remarked, "That's probably smart."

Joel snorted at what he probably thought was cowardice; but I ignored him, knowing the only way *he'd* venture into the basement would be if I — as usual — went first.

Seconds later, I stood in the middle of a musty smelling room. Wallpaper peeled from the walls in shriveled strips like used-up snakeskin, the floor covered with gritty dust, corners piled with crushed soda cans, broken beer bottles, a headless doll here, broken plate there.

An open door stood in the corner.

"So the stuff's in the other room?"

"Yeah," Joel drawled, "check it out…'less you're chicken."

Chris sighed as he climbed in after me. "You're an idiot."

Joel's reply was brilliant in its eloquence. "Bite me."

I ignored them, approaching the far room. A feeling lingered in the air, exerting a slight pressure I felt in my ears and head. Maybe all abandoned houses were like this, haunted by the memories of their former occupants.

Bassler House held more than memories.

I stepped through the door and stopped, arrested by what I saw.

In the room beyond was the much rumored pentagram – but it wasn't hastily scrawled on the wall, nor did it appear the work of drunken college students. Planted with the meticulous care of only the most committed was a brick-laid pentagram roughly the size of the room.

It was a near-perfect circle.

At that point, Chris reached my shoulder. "Holy…."

Still on the porch, Joel swiped a broken tree branch, wedged it between windowsill and window.

I glanced at him. "That's never been there before?"

Chris, breathless. "No *freakin'* way."

Joel, numb. "Uh-uh."

Of course, we did the next, most logical thing: we walked slowly around it.

Instantly, a putrid smell hit my nostrils, a high-pitched *buzz* I hadn't noticed before filling the air. Squinting, I saw above each pentagram triangle clouds of flies, and as I passed them, a rotten smell wafted upwards, making me taste bile.

Several *something*s had apparently been sacrificed here – or at the very least, someone wanted people to think so.

I never saw what rotted in those triangles, and to this day, I'm glad. I tell myself "squirrel" or "mouse", and I'm content.

We made our circuit and found ourselves clustered by a winding staircase leading to the second and third floors. The whiteness of my friend's faces told me enough: the pentagram was something they'd never seen before.

Stating the obvious, Chris whispered, "*This* is new."

I believed Chris's sincerity, but prodded Joel, who was prone to arranging elaborate pranks, "You didn't do this?"

The shock on his face was unnerving. Though Joel often talked with exaggerated flair, I can't easily call him a coward.

"No way," he muttered, corners of his mouth drawn tight.

Someone had painted the room's walls white, and the blankness felt alien, out of place. No junk collected here, and with the exception of the pentagram, the buzzing flies and decaying stench, the room was practically sterile.

However, as no black-robed Satanists slid from hidden crevices to offer us as virgin sacrifices, (which we'd be, despite our grandiose lies to each other), we relaxed. In our minds, we reasoned the pentagram was the creation of some lonely Goth kids with nothing better to do; the buzzing flies feasting on rotten hamburger, not animals. We couldn't explain the whiteness of the room, so we dismissed it.

Of course, the best thing to do in a situation like this is something stupid; because that always helps chase away cold sweats. After sharing very mundane explanations, Joel flashed his trademark grin. "We should wreck it."

I glanced at Chris. "You mean...."

"Sure. Toss the bricks out the window; screw up their little Goth-Satanist party." He raised his eye-brows pointedly. "God would *want* us to, dontcha think?"

If you've never been raised country-Baptist, such a challenge means nothing. However, both Joel and I had deacons for fathers, and though an Episcopalian, Chris had attended Afton Baptist with us for three years. The idea of God using us to smite the forces of lonely Goth Satan worshipers was absurd, yet oddly empowering.

This time I wasn't content to lead. "Fine," I nodded at the bricks, "be my guest."

Joel's eyes narrowed. For a moment, I thought he'd pass.

In a flash he grinned, vaulted to the pentagram, grabbed a brick, and flung it with rare enthusiasm at the room's only window.

The brick crashed through the glass with a righteous sound.

The next few minutes are hazy. When hordes of Satanists didn't stream forth to devour us, we descended upon the pentagram, driven, grabbing and chucking bricks through the window in a whirlwind of arms and legs.

I don't remember much but our flashing, twisted faces, howling mouths, burning eyes. We tossed, grabbed, threw – moving like manic machines.

I hate to think that in our fervor we scooped up the moldering, rotten masses in the pentagram's triangles with our bare hands, but we must've, because when the moment passed, the floor lay bare – though smeared in places.

Minutes later we stood in the room's center, panting, shirts soaked with sweat – though it wasn't hot. As our adrenaline ebbed, we eyed each other with dreadful fascination. We'd lost ourselves in the brick-throwing frenzy, the fervor of which was a bit alarming.

We stood there in the tired weirdness, waiting.

Joel broke the silence by clapping his hands with authority, saying, "Well, that's *that*. Let's go see if there's anything cool upstairs."

Suddenly, Bassler House returned to being nothing more than an old house in need of exploring. Our momentary fugue dismissed, we tramped up the winding stairs in search of more oddities.

Ten to fifteen minutes later, we descended, *disappointed*. We hadn't found much; most of the rooms were empty save scraps of litter, offering little amusement. Perhaps the most interesting things we'd found was a dented, pitted whisky flask in one room, and in another the entire floor had caved in, causing us to speculate if man or animal had plunged to their deaths through the gaping hole.

In the last room at the top of the stairs, we found a slightly chilling inscription that read…

On July 15th, 1975, Jessica Turnbuckle came here to party, drink, and have lots of sex. She passed out, and is now buried behind this wall.

…but that was a well known urban legend; something written in all abandoned houses - a bit spooky and nothing more.

I'm not sure how we didn't see it as we came down the stairs, but the *smell* hit us the instant our feet hit the bottom step.

"Holy *shit* …" Joel breathed.

There, in the middle of the room, was the pentagram, untouched, as if we'd never destroyed it. The flies buzzed as before, and when our collective eyes traveled to the window we'd thrown the bricks through….

"The window," I croaked, "it's not broken."

From our position, we saw the window we'd crawled through, and Chris pointed a shaking finger, managing, "The window we came in is closed."

"We left it open. Joel *propped* it open!"

I can tell you nothing of what happened next. Though we clambered towards our exit, seconds later we found ourselves standing around the pentagram, each at a triangle tip facing the other, rotten somethings *buzzing* at our feet with hordes of flies.

We couldn't move or speak; we stood clenched in fear. I'll never forget the sweaty sheen on Joel's forehead; the tendons straining in Chris's neck and my fingernails digging into my palms.

Nor will I forget the sinuous, slithering, shuffling, sliding coming from the far hallway, and though it lasted forever, it never got any closer.

Finally, Joel grated, "Wreck it. Gotta…*wreck it*."

They were magic words; breaking the spell. We again descended upon the pentagram. I remember our strange, twisted faces, howling mouths, burning eyes. We grabbed and threw bricks through the window *again.*

When we finished, Joel clapped his hands and said, "Well, that's *that.* Let's go see if there's anything cool upstairs."

Again we ascended, read the inscription about Jessica, descended, and when we hit bottom the stench of decayed meat assailed our nostrils as Joel breathed...

"Holy *shit.*"

"The window's not broken."

"Where we came in – it's *closed* Joel propped it open; I know he did!"

We tried to run, but found ourselves rooted again around the pentagram, as something slowly slid down the hallway – much closer this time.

We fought, struggled, sweat, ground our teeth until finally Joel managed, "Wreck it. Gotta...*wreck it.*"

Once again we did, only to find ourselves returned to our spots, the slithering and shuffling and sliding c*loser.*

After the same interminable fight, Joel choked, "Wreck it. Gotta...*wreck it.*"

I found my voice. "No! Leave it!"

Joel and Chris's heads turned stiffly towards me, eyes wide, disbelieving. "We have to," Joel hissed, "its making this happen!"

Something seized me; an increasing pressure banging inside my head. My ears rang and eyes watered, and I want to destroy the pentagram so bad my hands itched with desire.

The house didn't want me to talk. I don't know how I knew that, or how it was possible, but it was truth all the same.

I managed to shake my head stiffly. "No…it *wants* us to keep wrecking it…to stay stuck. It's holding us here…for *something*."

Shocked realization lit in their eyes. Chris nodded, wincing. "The sound in the hallway… it's getting closer."

My mind whirled and I felt sick; my head pounded and I tasted more bile, but I pressed on, following my intuition.

"We leave it," I gasped, fighting tears. "Go away, and we won't tell anyone about it."

"We'll forget."

The pressure disappeared; our bodies free.

The sounds in the hallway, however…*were closer*.

"Go!"

We pounded away from the pentagram, arms and legs pistoning, and into the adjoining room. With the loop broken the window was propped open as Joel had left it, but as we fled the slithering, sliding sound *filled* the room, and I'm sure each one of us – as I did – felt the hot mist of some dark creature's breath on our necks

Joel, faster than Chris and I, scrambled through the window first, knocked away the untrustworthy branch holding up the rickety window, bracing it open with his arm.

I've always wondered if he glimpsed what pursued us, because I remember his white face and dinner-plate eyes as he screamed, "*Its coming!*"

Chris made it through the window easily. I slid to a stop; my tall, lanky frame prone to clumsiness, and I easily saw myself bringing the window down upon me, shattered glass and all.

I put my hands and one foot on the windowsill to pull myself through…

…and stopped.

Suddenly, I wanted to turn around, and see *it* for what it was.

Something in me *needed* to.

Doing as they would for years to come – saving me from myself – Chris and Joel grabbed my shoulders and pulled me through the window. We crashed together on the old, weakened porch in a dusty heap, rotten boards groaning but not breaking. The window shut with a resounding *bang,* somehow not shattering.

The air fell still.

It was over.

We glanced at each other for several quiet minutes.

….won't tell a-anyone…

…we'll forget…

"We should get going," Chris offered, "Dad'll have the grill hot by now."

"Yeah," Joel added, "and Bonnie wanted to go into town before dinner."

I nodded, saying nothing. We got up, brushed the dust off our clothes, and walked away from Bassler House, ignoring the much lower sun; ignoring also the muted sound of something shuffling, slithering, sliding in the dark.

***

November, 2007

I sit back in my chair, flexing my fingers. My agent has bugged me for months about starting a novel, saying it's time to graduate from short stories. He says I've got *Bram Stoker Award* and Stephen King, Joe Hill, and Peter Straub written all over me.

This will never be published. I'd started it for myself, for understanding, closure, maybe meaning. It would make a great novel, but I'd already partly reneged on my promise, and didn't dare revoke it entirely.

...we'll forget...

When I don't write, I sleep well, but when I can't hold it inside any longer and I hold an evening confessional with my *Imac*, all through that night something shuffles and slides its way down the hallway towards my bedroom; shuffling, slithering, sliding, but never getting any closer. I imagine it'll stay that way, so long as I keep the rest of the promise.

We won't tell anyone.

I shut down the *Imac*, and head off to sleep – hoping to God the sliding won't come any closer tonight.

MR. FUCKING BOTHERSOME

By

Dave Rex

Imagine, if you will indulge it, our world without religion. Not, mind you, religion suddenly evaporating into nothing, but rather religion never having been birthed by the minds of its visionary, if perhaps self-serving, creators. Would there be any sort of naming conventions? There certainly would be no Johns, Lukes, Marys or the like. Would killing for the sake of sating urges or feeding hungers both physical and psychological then be acceptable or even expected? After all, it would make the individual stronger, more guarded and more cunning. Would the supposed "seven deadly sins", not being deadly sins without the advent of religion, then be committed with impunity or would we reap what we sow? Could the individual, or indeed even the whole of society, be moral without being instructed in the virtues of right and wrong; benevolence and malevolence? The following is a story of one man's last day in such a world.

* * * *

My name has been Beard for about a month now. I've had a pretty nasty cough lately and it's fucking bothersome, so I'm going to off myself today.

I woke up earlier this morning than I had intended. I'm pretty sure it was because my girlfriend lying next to me in bed was sound asleep, snoring so very loudly. I found that to be fucking bothersome, though I do love her dearly. It's easy to love when all apprehension is swept aside; it's easy to do a great many things then. She looked so peaceful there, motionless and naked, the rays of early dawn capturing her small, pert breasts like an oeuvre in a fine art gallery.

My throat burned with the need for drink, but the heat of my semi-hard cock held a different desire altogether. I coughed loudly and raggedly as I began stroking my cock to the illuminated view of my lovely girlfriend. She stirred at the sound of my hacking cough and then rolled over onto her stomach. Her alabaster ass was so ample, so very inviting. I straddled her and smacked first one, then the other ass cheek. She awoke and craned her neck to look at me with stunning blue eyes. "Someone's in an amorous mood this morning," she cooed. She rested her chin on the knuckles of her delicate folded hands and wiggled her ass teasingly. I smacked those perfect ass cheeks again and delighted at their new redness. My cock grew to full hardness and twitched at the brilliant sting on my palm.

I plunged into her tiny anus, though I do not recall the moment of penetration. She accepted my thick offering dutifully, if not wantonly, and without a whimper. I thrust in and out but a few times, as I recollect, before cuming. It felt…ok. This animalistic act was about me and my urges; my giving over fully to instinct. Were this her moment, I would take my time if she so desired, or ravish her if that were her need. I would eat out her pussy with loving care or simply lie there as she straddled me and rode me like some anatomically correct, malleable mannequin.

I collapsed atop my dear, loving girlfriend and planted a gentle kiss on her soft right shoulder before rolling over. It was not long before she fell back to sleep. I laid there on my side and my eyes and thoughts drifted to those ample ass cheeks. They looked absolutely...edible, the red swelling atop vanilla flesh like sweet strawberry syrup covering a mound of luscious gelato; confection for baby's sweet tooth. My pleasant, child-like respite was interrupted by her resumed shrill snoring. That was fucking bothersome.

I reached into my nightstand and withdrew a pocket knife, which I kept handy for protection, but only ever had to make use of a few times really, aside from the skinning of...various things. I rolled back over to face my darling, loving sweetheart and whispered "I love you." as the blade glinted in the morning sunlight and made a deep, narrow slit across her creamy throat. *I didn't want her to miss me when I was gone. I owed her that much.* I kissed her soft, ruby red lips. I thought she might scream, or attempt to, but she did not. She awoke, wide-eyed for ten, maybe fifteen seconds. I pinned her down by those delicate, alabaster shoulders and reveled in her sudden, extended, all-consuming tension; that not-so-gentle reminder that you are slipping into the numb nothingness of death. It made my cock harden again. Finally, she eased into that eternal sleep. She did not snore.

Slowly, I slipped away from the beautiful pallor corpse beside me and wandered lazily into the bathroom. My throat and my chest hurt all the more so after yet another fit of coughing. I instinctively reached for the aspirin bottle, but then pulled my hand back. Come pleasure or pain, I was resolute to feel every minute gradation while I still could feel. The utter end of me was coming today and there would be nothing from that moment on.

I found myself absentmindedly scratching madly at my plump beard to relieve an itch that had recently proven fucking bothersome. I proceeded to shave off the beard and delighted in the stings of several nicks from the razor. My beard--my most recent identity--cleanly removed, I needed a new moniker. When I hacked up a cough that produced a viscous, bloody discharge and a pain that felt like I had just slammed into a brick wall, I became Mr. Fucking Bothersome for this, the last day of my existence. Why not? It fits like shit in the bowels.

I took a long, hot shower, pissing down the drain and then jerking off to the vision of my murdered love and those inviting, porcelain-like ass cheeks still sharp in my brain. The blood on my hands---the result of my gift to my love--washed off easily under the pulsating pressure of the shower and the permeating steam granted a much deserved respite for my nagging cough. It was not fair, after all, that I should be made to suffer so when so many others were not. I opted not to wear any clothing this day. I would die as I was born, minus the incessant--and fucking bothersome--crying. Some wore clothing for the sake of vanity or warmth or even to cover curves and bulges that might otherwise inflame the baser dispositions of those they did not carnally desire. Many, however, roamed naked and emancipated, celebrating the natural beauty of the human form and, more often than not, wanted to be ravaged without warning like beasts in the wild.

I picked up the gore-slathered pocket knife that still lay on the twisted bed sheet next to the love of my life and flayed a generous portion of the inviting flesh from both sides of her bounteous posterior. I carried the two bloody slabs of meat back to the bathroom and rinsed off the gore in the sink. I looked in the mirror above the sink and watched myself take profound pleasure in the tender, salty-sweet flavor of my darling's ass flesh. It was better, I dare say, than I had fantasized it to be. Perhaps it was because I truly did love her so very deeply and because she so very deeply delighted in callous, faceless anal sex.

I gobbled up the second piece rather greedily, yet still suffered sharp pangs of hunger. That was fucking bothersome. I moved quickly to the kitchen, pocket knife ever in hand, guided by a yearning to sate my animal ravenousness. I ate everything in the kitchen. *Hunted for and tore at* everything in the kitchen like some great bear fresh from hibernation. I even got into the cat food. Then, as I popped kibble into my gullet as though it were hot, buttery popcorn, it dawned on me. Why eat kibble when I could use it to lure lively prey?

"Here kitty, kitty," I called out as I emptied what remained of the kibble into Prince's porcelain white bowl. He came strutting into the kitchen from the living room, stretching his slim limbs and purring a contented, lazy purr, no doubt wakening for the first time today, lured by the familiar resonance of food tinkling against the hollow interior of his bowl. Prince chowed down with ravenous abandon, his head bobbing up and down in a blur of motion like a hooker in a hurry.

I watched him eat as I gently stroked his smooth coat and you know what? I do believe my darling sweetheart loved that useless, freeloading little shit more than she loved me. I found that to be more than a little fucking bothersome. I grabbed his royal fucking Highness by the scruff of his neck. He instantly twisted, clawed, meowed and hissed wildly in protest and even managed a few swipes along my exposed chest. I thrust the creature out at arm's length, not because I did not relish the cuts from his thrashing, but to gain optimal control. I banged the pathetic creature's cranium against one edge of the kitchen counter as though I were loosening the stem on a head of lettuce. He still thrashed a bit, or spasmed. All the same to me. Two more solid skull whacks against the counter and the once foppish feline was finally dead.

I wasted no time in splitting Prince open from nape to groin with my handy dandy pocket knife. He was surprisingly yielding to my blade for such a wiry little fucker. I then skinned him with a savage precision I was not aware I had. I separated meat from bone and laid the meat out on a cast iron skillet like tiny, tender cutlets. I turned on the stove and added a few spices from the cupboard as well as some slabs of butter from the fridge and several splashes of hot sauce for a bit of a kick. The meat sizzled as I shifted it about with a spatula to keep it from sticking to the skillet. That triggered an aroma. Oh fuck! Such an aroma! It made my mouth water with anticipation and my belly rumble with demand.

I walked the skillet and a bottle of whiskey into the living room and sat down on my favorite leather lounge chair, seething with revitalization at the burning of my right hand on the searing skillet handle. I ate Prince with my hands. I wanted to feel my nourishment. There was something…natural about it. Like catching a live fish from a rapidly flowing river with your bare hands or killing someone with only your hands. I wondered then, as dribbles of greasy juice trickled down my chin, how it would have felt to strangle my beloved rather than slitting her delicate, pale throat like I did. But I would not wish her such a prolonged, uncomfortable death. No. There would be someone walking this city's streets deserving of a lengthy strangulation by my powerful hands and I would most assuredly find enormous pleasure in delivering such a punishment sometime before taking my own life.

I turned on the television to the Extreme Sports channel. The war was on. It had been for about a month now, but at least we were ahead in points by a suitable margin. The spectacle was live and the sports announcer was recapping the reasons for this most recent conflict. *We* were at war with *them* because *we* were jealous of *their* over abundance of oil which was supposedly desperately needed by *us* to keep *our* great machine running and *they* were at war with *us* because *they* were jealous of *our* over abundance of personal freedoms. Blah, blah, blah. I hated that droning, toupee wearing pussy of an announcer. He was so fucking bothersome. I thought about skinning and gutting him too before the day was over as I gnawed on the animal flesh from the skillet. Asshole sports announcer aside, the war did make for a first-rate bit of visceral entertainment while I sucked the greasy juice from my fingers. Prince tasted, surprisingly enough, a lot like chicken. "Finger lickin' chicken," I said aloud with a chuckle. It felt good to laugh. I really should have done it more often.

Once I had finished the last morsels of the late Prince and washed them down with a long pull from the whisky bottle, the fucking sports announcer was flapping his yap again. I hurled the hefty skillet at the television screen that I would no longer have need of and delighted as the announcer's bulbous head blew up in a shower of sparks and tiny glass shards. A smattering of the tiny shards sliced into my legs and crotch and my cock got hard with a sharp intake of breath.

There was nothing left to do or be done here within these four walls. This solid cube of a prison which held no more aberrant distractions for one such as me. I got up from my chair, which in itself had become far too comfortable and familiar for my liking--my *newfound* predilection. I walked to the door and jerked it open. Both the warm and the cool of early autumn hit my naked flesh like a blanket of ecstasy. I arched my back and then twisted from side to side, stretching my muscles and tweaking my bones. Pocket knife in my singed right hand, a half-full bottle of whisky in my left and the remains of a greasy kill on my face, I walked out into the day. The city was big, its citizens bold. But now, the city was my playground, its citizens my playthings. It was time to see just what fucked up shit I could get into before I offed myself at day's end.

Like a feral cat, I scanned the immediate playground around me, searching for the first living thing that asked to be preyed upon with their actions. I had found my ideal target. He was an old man. He sat lazily in a wheelchair wasting space and greedily sucking oxygen from a canister, wasting a natural resource. He was being pushed across the street by a pretty, young nurse, again wasting a natural resource - she was dressed from head to toe in white, but such standoffish wrapping would not stop me from tearing her open and partaking of her sweetness if I so chose.

The elderly lump of sickness in the wheelchair should have been hunted and killed a long time ago, but he was the owner of a major corporation, and so he continued to live. His name, in fact, was Owner. With such an audacious name, perhaps he felt he possessed everything and everyone. I found that to be absolutely fucking bothersome. Owner, I should also mention, *was* my boss.

He was surrounded on all sides by four bodyguards in fine, identical suits and opaque sunglass. They carried no guns or stunning devices of any kind, for such weapons were banned in this city for a period of six months. This, due to the escalating imbalance in the hunting grounds of civility. It had been deemed unethical, as it had periodically for ages, for citizens to attempt a life without being equally armed, and the affluent would easily and regularly out advance the less fortunate in that regard. Personally, I feel wealth breeds weakness and a toxic sense of security, whereas paucity propagates rigid self-awareness and endurance. Many others feel the same way, and so the ban would be lifted after only six months and then reinstated once the imbalance again grew too great.

The quartet of bulky bodyguards looked onward, never behind. It was immoral, you see, to pursue your prey from the rear. Ah, but what retribution have I to fear, my family long dead and my only love recently freed from her own corporeal shell? Since I am to commit self-murder by day's end, whose wrath should I concern myself with beyond that of the carrion eaters of my inert flesh? Morality is personal conscience and, after all, is just that, *personal*.

I approached silently and stealthily from behind, unseen and unheard. I was one among many, yet uniquely qualified for and morally justified in what I was about to do. In one low, fluid motion, I yanked the oxygen tube from the canister attached to the back of Owner's wheelchair with my left hand while slashing the Achilles tendon of the bodyguard nearest me with the switchblade knife in my right hand. He belted out a growl of pain and fell almost immediately to one knee as blood flowed from the sudden wound, painting the street in viscous crimson trails. Two of the remaining bodyguards clumsily stumbled over the fallen one, trying to get to me, while the last one worked frantically and incredibly ineptly at getting the oxygen tube reconnected to the canister. These guardians were not predators. No. They were like obedient, brainless dogs, barking and chomping at the bit for a few scraps from their owner, *Owner*.

I did not expect to be the catalyst of so much gratifying chaos by means of such untried grace, of course. Before today, I had not the presence of mind to see such a ballsy action through, truth be told. It truly is wondrous just what one is capable of when repercussions are of no concern. An unfettered liberation of the mind and the body.

Owner fought desperately for air that would not accommodate him and I watched in awe and with bated breath until that breath was knocked out of me by the ungainly tackling of the two bodyguards. As they pounded on me, so did Owner's wrinkled, liver spotted, arthritic hands on the padded armrests of his wheelchair. I took pleasure in the pain come unto me as I did in that old fucker's long suffering struggle for life.

Chaos can spread like a virus due to a breakdown in *perceived* strength and a man like Owner has many enemies. One by one, citizens converged on the scene of chaos I had so proudly wrought. Some watched and waited like hyenas sensing weakness as the two bodyguards punched and kicked me with abandoned, tiring themselves out. Others bided their time to strike as the one dumbly obedient pet of a guardian continued to fiddle with the oxygen tube, not realizing that Owner - *his owner* - had already died; and the fourth loyal guard dog lay motionless, slowly bleeding out his life with no owner around to tell him what to do or even give a shit.

I watched in smug satisfaction as many in the gathered crowd began beating on the four distracted, dying and done-in bodyguards and still more stabbed wildly with sharp weapons of all kinds. Blood poured onto the street and muffled screams filled the morning air. It was beautiful. Vibrant. Natural. And I rose gradually to my feet just as the guard dogs went down in slaughtered piles of clothing and corpus. I felt no remorse. No pain, though I was profoundly conscience of its presence. I saw a pigeon and was taken away from the chaos by its freedom of boundless flight. I had found my next prey as well as my next meal. The gift of flight is wasted on birds.

I followed my new prey on an awkward path which eventually led to an alleyway. It landed on an open dumpster and busied itself with something inside. I snuck up on it and grabbed it with one nimble hand by the tail feathers just as it sensed my presence and attempted to once again take flight. It cooed, though not softly, and beat its wings wildly as I clasped my free hand over its chest. I felt calm and even a little aroused at the feel of a warm, palpitating heart and the sensation of biting into the bulk of living prey was...*delicious*.

As my teeth sunk into the pigeon flesh and warm blood trickled down my chin, two men and a woman approached naked from out of the alleyway's darkest recesses. They were the personification of filth. They rushed on me with broken bottles in hand and I could already smell on their collective breaths the cheap booze those bottles once contained. I continued my lustful feast knowing it could very well be my last. As they entered into the light of day, I could see their grim and abscess covered bodies, their ragged, lice ridden hair and their scattering of brown and black teeth. The trio could sense my vulnerability and desire not to fight back. *What will come, will come.* One of them held my feet down for good measure while the woman sat on my face. I gagged on the intensely invasive odor of fish and shit as I felt one of the broken bottles steadily slice a large square at the center of my chest. And they ate of me...*and the sensation of biting into the bulk of living prey was...delicious.* I realized, as the trio swallowed and then cut into me more, that I had not coughed once since leaving my apartment.

Suddenly, the pain became very *real* to me. "Help me!" I screamed to whomever would listen. Of course, no one would.

NOT A CHANCE

By

Jessica Lynne Gardner

Spam. He had been eating it for over two months now, some kind of meat shortage in Canada they said. Of course, he knew what really happened but he wasn't talking and neither were the livestock. He speared a piece of pink, flaky, salt-soaked animal byproduct and turned it with an impersonal plastic fork, disliking the way the long florescent beams reflected so harshly on its cold, black surface. In fact he made a mental note to do something about it when he got out of there, drive a truck through the place and demand that everyone be given real silverware or hell, even chopsticks-anything but the damned plastic. To make things worse the fish tank was overcrowded and they threw in another newbie. His back cracked loudly as he moved; the floor hadn't been kind to him this past week. The other two were talking too loud, making his head pound angrily.

"Hey man, so what's your poison?" The tightly stretched voice, still sounding nearly pre-pubescent despite his age, had come from the new kid. He looked about twenty-two with a spacer in his left ear and his pale head shaved clean, making the same reflection as the fork.

Sean enjoyed it when fish like this asked. He stared, unflinching, at the other's wide-eyed gaze and demanded, "What do you think?"

The kid sat in silence, appraising the older man's un-kept dark beard and wavy, shoulder length mane. Deeply set blue eyes peered over a sharp nose which, by the crooked position of the bones, had been broken a few times. He could almost feel the boy tremble.

"Well I uh, I'm not…"

"Name?"

"Uh, Kevin".

Sean nodded. He liked this kid, he had some guts, wasn't as stupid as the last fish they had. "It's not what you think it is… I didn't kill anybody, or at least I don't think I did." He felt the boy's eyes on him as he said the last part and nearly smiled despite himself. "But I'll tell you my sad little tale if I can have that chain around your neck."

"No man, what are you crazy?" Kevin's hand went up to protect a silver rope-chain, grasping the large sterling crucifix pendant in his skeletal fist.

"Don't worry son, the shit that guy will fill your head with is worth it; like watchin' a damned movie. Only entertainment you can get in here." Tom had been here for three weeks now and was steadily growing on him.

"So what do you say? Entertainment or boredom?" Sean asked.

"Yeah, well, I'll be the judge of how entertaining it is. Why do you want silver anyway? Not like you can get anything for it in here."

Sean laughed softly at his remark before going quiet again, his face solemn. "For protection."

"Oh Jesus, here we go again," Tom said, shaking his head.

"You ever really look up at a full moon, kid?"

Kevin shrugged. "Not really, maybe when I was younger once…" he mumbled.

"You should. There is power in that thing. It calls out the wild beast in us, drawing them out of the night where our sins can no longer hide…"

Kevin laughed. "Whoa, you really are crazy. I think you're in the wrong kind of jail-"

Before he finished Sean leapt up and showed him a jagged red scar dragged across his chest.

He stared at the deep imprints of a massive claw that trailed from his right shoulder down to his left side.

"Shit…what the hell happened to you…get hit by a bear or somethin'?"

"Ha, that's right, tell him, kid! Finally got a doubter, Sean. May not get that silver after all."

Kevin smiled nervously. "Yeah, Tom, that's right. I ain't a fool. People actually believed this guy?"

Sean zipped his orange uniform back up and sat back down against the wall. He reached behind him and took out a small wooden box, opening the hinge. Inside were two chains with an ankh and cross pendant and one ring with the blue star of Solomon etched in the middle; only jewelry with religious symbols were allowed in the cells. Closing it he put it almost reverently back in its place.

"I didn't believe in them myself until I saw them first hand."

"What's this about vampires and ghosts and bullshit?"

"Werewolves to be exact. Quite a few of them."

Kevin scratched his hairless head and walked away with his hands raised, "I don't have to listen to bullshit stories anymore-"

"Why do you think we have a live-stock crisis on our hands all of a sudden? You think all of the cows and chickens suddenly started killing each other? The animals aren't diseased or dead, they're missing."

The kid stood soberly, chewing the inside of his lip.

"Got a point there," added Tom unnecessarily as he reclined in his bunk, hands behind his head.

"Why would they kill animals, but not people?"

Sean gave a mirthless laugh. "Oh they do and they will. I can tell you plenty of things I've seen them do. The problem is that they have more intelligence than we give them credit for. They know if people start disappearing in the same numbers that these animals have then they are going to have a problem."

The kid sighed and sat down cross legged on the floor.

"Whatever..." he mumbled, tired of arguing and a little afraid of what the man might do if he voiced his disagreement.

Sean bowed his head and put an arm around his knees in thought, his eyes half closed as he the memory returned with more details than he would have liked.

"Before all of this started I was a livestock maintenance man for major fast food corporations. Not a bad job- as long as you're not the sensitive type. My tasks were pretty basic: feed, water, remove the dead ones. Nothing remarkable ever happened, so sometimes the guys would get bored, toss around a chicken or two during their shift and go home. Well, one day, about three or four weeks on the job, something finally happened. The chicken corpses began appearing first... We thought it was bad feed. The water, food, even the damn air was tested, but nothing turned up positive. So like most livestock corporations we ignored it and sure enough, the bodies were fewer for a while.

"The shifts returned to normal and we assumed it was just a few sickly birds. Then we noticed the same thing happening with the cows and pigs. It got worse and worse until no corpses were appearing at all, just stains marking where they were killed. Everyone was called in for questioning, myself included. Needless to say, no one had any explanations. Some sick joke was being played and we were getting the blame.

"So, naturally, the cameras were put up and again we saw dead ends. Whoever it was must have been smarter than some juvenile punk as we had originally thought. But no one could understand why they did it... I mean, it would be different if there were hundreds of animals stolen but why groups of twenty at a time? And why would they kill them first? It didn't make any sense.

"One of the workers, Hernandez, was convinced that this was the work of the Chupacabras, a legend in Mexico. He said it was a demon that would attack goats and farms, drinking the blood of the animals like a vampire. But the description he provided didn't match up. A creature that small wouldn't be able to take on a full grown heifer by itself assuming that the ridiculous story were real in the first place..."

Kevin snickered. "Oh so the Chupacabras is fake but werewolves are real…"

Sean glared at him a moment before continuing.

"Next week the camera equipment was found in a million pieces scattered across the ground. The tape had been shredded into barely recognizable strips. So we were dealing with a psycho, some kind of loony criminal who had something against livestock or who was really hungry."

Tom gave a hearty laugh at this but Kevin sat unreadable.

Either way, the only choice the company had was to place guards inside which they were outraged in doing, the cost for the animals wasn't nearly as much as the fee for the guards. So they put two guys in there with a pair of pistols and locked the place up again. I guess you can guess what happened next…?"

"Nothin' happened," Kevin stated with a bored look on his face.

"One of them was torn to pieces and the other well, they never found the other."

Kevin raised his brows at this and leaned forward.

"So we had no choice except to send all the livestock out to another branch while the police came in and wiped up the mess."

"So how'd you get that scar?"

Sean closed his eyes and swallowed hard. "I wanted to see who was behind this thing. I waited in my truck until after all of the police had gone and took a fresh piece of cow loin and a rifle with me. I sat the meat in front of the doors and went inside, watching from the crack between them. I waited for about three hours until I heard something. I heard the sound of eating and looked between the space of the doors…", he stopped and shook his head.

"Did you see it, what did it look like?" Kevin asked nervously.

"Kid, you wouldn't believe me if I told you in detail how it looked. Suffice to say, the thing was easily seven feet and mean. My breathing must have got heavier 'cause he looked through the slot with those yellow eyes, tore open the doors and ripped my chest, giving me this scar."

"Didn't you say you had a rifle? Shit! Why didn't you kill the bastard?"

"After he sliced me I gave him a good shot in the shoulder. It was enough to scare him off but not to hurt it too bad. That's why I'm collecting this silver. I'm gonna be ready when they come for me. After that I went out and stole a few silver bars, they caught me and that's the end of that part of the story."

The boy, who had been chewing his fingernails in anticipation for last few minutes, stopped after he said this. "You think the creatures would come back just for you?"

Sean nodded slowly, "They've smelled my blood. But it doesn't matter, I'm not going to give them a chance. I'm gonna kill those bastards for what they did...sometimes I think they may have killed my Tabitha. She disappeared shortly after my encounter in the barn."

Kevin laughed nervously. "You're full of shit man. But I'll give you credit though, that's the best story I've heard in awhile. You should send it to a movie director or somethin'."

Sean wasn't smiling.

"Well I don't know. If what you say is true I better just hold on to my silver then," Kevin said with a smirk.

"It's not going to do you much good unless it's shaped into a bullet now is it?"

Kevin's smirk disappeared. "Look, we are going to be in this cell for awhile bro and I don't see any ways of making bullets around here."

Sean glared it him for a moment then shrugged, "That's up to you, but I am getting out of here pretty soon."

Both Tom and the kid stared at him hard when he said this.

"What are you talking about, Sean? You've been in here for at least two months. If you could get out why didn't you go sooner? Don't listen to him kid, his head's in the clouds."

Sean smiled. It was a smug kind of smile, not friendly in the least. He looked up at the cameras and positioned his body to block its view. He put a finger up to his lips and pulled a piece of sharpened metal that resembled a knife out of his sock. Once they got a good look at it he put it back.

"There are three guards that run the graveyard shift on this level. Those are the ones we need to take care of."

"Hey now, I'm too old for this shit. How the hell did you get that? I'm in here for three more months, I don't want to be put away for life," Tom said, sitting straighter in his cot, his nearly hairless eyebrows making slanted lines over his deep-set blue eyes. "Could you imagine if we screwed up? We'd be tried for tryin' to escape and for killing prison guards. That sentence wouldn't be too light, buddy."

Kevin turned away from Tom and watched the other, looking straight into his expressionless gaze. Sean stared back.

"What's the gist?"

"I say we wait for another hour and a half when they come in to check on us for lights out. One of you start making some noises like you're in pain and he'll come closer. Then, we stick him through."

"That don't sound like a very good plan to me, son," Tom said with a little laugh.

Kevin nodded. "Yeah that's what they do in all those prison movies."

"That's why we are going to have to make this more believable. I've been watching their habits since my first day in. This is a newer prison with young guards that do a half-ass job because they could care less about making the streets any safer. Now, one of you needs to volunteer to be stuck first. Nothing major," he emphasized, holding up a palm, "Just a little prick in the shoulder or leg or somewhere, we need some blood."

"You're crazy. If you think I'm gonna bleed for this shit, you're wrong," Kevin scoffed.

Tom nodded. "Sorry Sean, but it looks like you have to be the volunteer."

Sean placed his hand on his ankle where the sock was and leaned back against the wall stretching his legs out in front of him and closing his eyes. The other two exchanged glances.

They waited until Sean was asleep then they moved as close to the corner as possible to talk. "You think this guy is for real?" asked Kevin, gesturing with a tilt of his bald head toward the sleeping man.

"Naw, he's full of it, that one. I wouldn't trust him in a second. He'll have us both put away for good, he will."

Kevin nodded, "Yeah, let him oversleep."

Thirty-five minutes later, Sean heard Kevin creeping over to him. He kept his eyes closed tightly. He felt the blade slip out of his sock and nearly smiled. He heard the muffled sound of Tom's scream from under the pillow as the knife went through his chest.

Looks like you chose the wrong side, Tom, my friend...

The guard's footsteps echoed coldly down the hall. *Ah, perfect timing...,* he thought. He felt the kid staring at him, knew what he was planning. That boy was as twisted as they come and Tom hadn't been a saint either.

The footsteps were getting closer. He waited, hearing the hesitant steps of Kevin moving toward him. Then he heard the light switch click. He jumped up and began screaming. The guard switched the light back on and ran over to them. He saw Tom's form sprawled in the corner, blood seeping through the Orange jumpsuit and soaking into the once off-white cot underneath.

"Jesus Christ..." the guard started to reach for his walkie-talkie.

"Sir please, he still has the knife, he tried to kill me!" pleaded Sean, eyes wide and visibly trembling all over.

Kevin stood blankly with the knife in hand.

Good boy, play dumb.

The guard was young. He left the radio in his belt and whipped out his keys, rushing to unlatch the gate.

He went toward Kevin who dropped his knife at the sight of the gun. Sean moved fast. He grabbed a second knife, only this one was much sharper, out of his other sock and stabbed the guard in the back while holding a hand over his mouth to muffle the sound. He stabbed him a few times, making sure he would go fast.

The boy didn't miss a beat. He took the guard's gun and pointed it at Sean. "How did you know?"

"I'm not really in here for stealing silver bars and it looks like I'm not the only one who has played the con-artist game in my lifetime. Now let's go. You need me," Sean whispered.

He picked up the guard's keys and they headed out. A few seconds down the hall, an alarm began shrieking. The kid cursed in frustration.

"No- wait, that's not an escape alarm. It's a fire alarm."

"What? You sure?"

Sean nodded. "Yeah, I heard the escape alarm two weeks ago when someone from another cell got out. This isn't it."

They took off, deciding to use the distraction to their advantage.

When they reached the middle of the long cellblock, they heard a loud crash from the floor above them.

"Where are all the guards? I mean if this is a fire shouldn't there be more guards to transfer us all to another prison or somethin'?"

Sean clenched his jaw. The kid was right. "Just keep going. Whatever it is it should be bad enough to keep them occupied."

Sean started to sweat; he could feel the fear eating his innards as surely as the werewolves would if they caught him. An image of

Tabitha's face flashed in his mind. It was right after they had decided to get engaged.

He still remembered what she was reading that night, Bram Stoker's Dracula. He never understood how she could love such horror. Even though he would never admit it, he had always feared the dark. If she were alive she would have loved the idea of werewolves roaming the city. His eyes stung for just a second, *if she were alive...*

He fueled his sadness into hatred as they began to move faster through the ugly, bland halls of the prison. A few of the inmates yelled and rattled things against the cages as they sped by, hoping to escape. At the end of the hall there was a guard with deep lacerations on his neck and chest, the crimson pool around him reflecting the beams of the elongated fluorescent bulbs. Sean shivered a chill working down his spine.

"You ok?"

Sean looked at him and nodded, Christ he hated those damn bulbs... if he didn't escape tonight he promised himself he would smother in his own pillow tomorrow.

"So far so good...whoever it was did all the work for us already."

Kevin looked at the body and swallowed hard, his huge eyes dilating in the dark. A trail of narrow blood rivers showed them the way. Up a little further was a flight of stairs. They hurried down the non-remarkable white stairs speckled with tiny, sporadic tan spots. Sean remembered the last time he saw them. He recalled envisioning escape plans even as he had first walked through the door of the prison. He felt the anger, the hatred, the pride...he pushed his memory to go back further. He saw the handcuffs, gleaming metal stained with red, clasp his wrists in front of him. He saw the look on the officer's face... the self-righteous judgment in his frown. He struggled, trying to see the rest of the scene. The edges of the memory snapshot became blurred until it vaporized into nothing.

Kevin knitted his brows together as he watched the play of emotions surfacing in the other's face. They stopped on the second set of stairs. As they stared at the lower level it was impossible to see anything but the red. Before them was a blood-painted three-dimensional portrait of the darkest vision either of them had even witnessed. The bodies were un-recognizable, a tangled mass of internal organs lying beside them. Kevin began gagging, but Sean just stared, the whole scene seemed so familiar.

After relieving his nausea all over the floor, Kevin gave Sean a gesture toward the door and they walked out of the prison. Once outside Sean laughed. He looked up. *No more bulbs...* There weren't any stars but that was ok, because the moon would have blotted them out anyway.

It was the hunter's moon, close enough to touch and tinged slightly with red. Kevin was trembling. "God dammit! You never had a plan did you? If it weren't for..." he paused with difficulty, "for them bein' dead then we would have been caught. What could have done that? I don't think a human could have done that."

Sean wasn't listening to his ramblings. He heard a twig snap in the bushes and regained his composure.

"Let's go," Sean demanded.

They began casually moving in the other direction, toward a small forest.

"I don't think we should go in there, man, those things might be hidin' in there."

"It's either that or give the investigators witnesses that saw two prisoners stained with blood walking the streets."

Kevin nodded reluctantly and followed. The forest was more like a dark dale with enough trees to make it shadowed yet still have a clear view of the sky.

"Now what? It ain't like we could survive in this place for long. Shouldn't we be going far away from here?" Kevin asked.

"The plan is to wait it out until tomorrow and then get a bus headed out of state…" his words were distracted as he watched the shadows.

Kevin narrowed his eyes, watching his movements with suspicion. "Hey-", the kid said firmly, "Hey I'm talkin' to you!" He grabbed the older man's jumpsuit collar, "Did you set me up? Huh? Are you gettin' paid for this?"

Out of the corner of his eye he saw a tall dark shape step out of the trees. The kid turned at a painfully slow speed, fear gripping his heart. It was thin and gangly with tufts of matted ivory fur which was missing in some places, revealing yellowed, stitched human skin underneath. Walking on two hind feet, each digit complete with sharp silver claws, it stopped in front of them, the moonlight splashing on the snarling jaws. Kevin backed away nearly tripping himself and looked desperately at Sean who couldn't tear his gaze from the creature.

Their gaze was locked; the deep, amber-chestnut eyes of the monster and the measured blue of the man. The growling quieted and it started licking its chops, its eyes lowering in an almost submissive state.

Sean moved toward it, his hand beginning to lift as if to touch the animal, "T-Tabbie?"

A small whine emitted from its throat. Glowing eyes in the dark dale behind it began to come closer but one sharp growl and they remained in place.

"No- you can't be my Tabitha... she's dead," his voice was thick with an unspoken threat of tears. "Go back to your forest, demon," he said turning his back on it. "My Tabbie is no more and I'll not have anyone or anything defile her memory." The tears were no longer waiting and leaked down his cheeks along with the memories.

Kevin, who had been quietly watching behind the nearest tree, pointed a shaking finger toward the monster behind him and Sean reluctantly turned to face it.

It let out loud growls, its teeth clamping open and shut in threat. Then it closed its eyes and appeared to be seizing. When it stopped and opened its eyes, Sean saw the eyes of his beloved; clear, dark eyes filled with sorrow. "Sh-sh-Sean...", she stuttered, sounding like a child who has learned to speak.

"What happened?" was all he could manage.

She looked at him bewildered, "You don't rem-remember...?"

The wave was almost too much for him to handle. Within one second the last fifteen years of his life made itself known to him in visions of blood, tears and pain. He sank down to the ground, holding his head as if trying to keep it from exploding. He saw visions of Tabbie lying on the ground, the heart failure had only taken a few moments to kill her. He saw himself in agony, then in anger, then in resolution, searching through books and scrolls and files. He saw the table with her still body, the wolf's warm heart going into the hole inside her chest.

"No... no", he whispered. "I worked for meat suppliers I wasn't a scientist..."

"Lies," she said softly, "Intricate stories you made up to tell the police. You had starting going mad toward the end..."

"What about this scar...?"

Before he finished his sentence, it all appeared before him in overwhelming images. Tabitha had been newly reborn in all her glory and he was training her just as he had the others. He had wanted her to be the guinea pig. The young Pit bull tied to the pole wouldn't have had a chance, not a chance... but she had refused. She was whimpering. He felt the rage he had for her, then. How dare she disobey her savior, her *creator?* He struck her beautifully sowed face. He thought it a shame to ruin such handiwork yet continued to hit again and again, each time harder than the next until the blood flowed from the tightly stitched seams of her skin. A silver claw rose up in defense, easily slicing open his chest. Falling back, he grunted as his struck his head on the ground.

He stood up, now fully in the present, his normally calm sounding voice filled with arrogance. "You ungrateful bitch! How could you do that to me? You turned me in didn't you?" he demanded.

Kevin appeared beside him in amazement. "Shit, you- you created werewolves? You can control them..." he said in awe at the subdued monsters before him.

"No matter," he said, ignoring Kevin's comment, his voice rising. "We shall soon be getting back to our training. Then we will take what's ours and be rid of this weak, human race. We'll make a race worth saving, one that can live without fear of fragile mortality."

With that he took out a knife and stuck it deep into the boy's chest. Kevin groaned, gasping as the pain overtook him in flashing bursts inside his skull then throughout his nerve endings like a strand of bursting Christmas lights.

"Here is your first order. Finish him off."

Silence. He turned to her, taking out the bloody knife and holding it in front of her, "I warn you..." Silence.

The golden-eyed creatures that were waiting behind her suddenly appeared, stalking out of the night. They stood behind their leader, tongues sliding over jagged, canine teeth impatiently as their fur bristled. Their sights were set for the kill. Tabitha shot them a sharp glance. She winced but knew she was ready. Salivating, she hungered for the raw, beating heart inside him. The others had their share now it was her turn.

Seeing her advance, Sean swallowed, raising his hands slowly to ward her off. She moved in, oblivious to his screams. It didn't take her long to rip her maker apart; this was only her first time but as her powerful jaws bit down into his chest he didn't have a chance, not a chance...

Available now at <u>www.lulu.com</u>

ROUGH NIGHT FOR GLADYS

By

Colin M. Maguire

The whole afternoon had been bad, getting colder and meaner as the storm picked up. Damp and icy – the winds and sleet punched through the city like an aggressive drunk. The entire week had grown progressively worse, but today's abrasive gloom had undisputedly signaled that winter was barreling headlong into town - and you had better run for cover, if you knew what was good for you. Today's cold was biting, and looking for victims.

To Gladys, the chill day resembled Death itself. Death, in a word.

She could taste the very essence of the Reaper, set upon the wicked autumn wind - creeping up on her with steady certainty. It was riding in on a gray horse of overcast and rain. Riding in and scattering colored, dying leaves in its wake, littering the park beyond - leaving the mean, cracked sidewalks swathed in varicolored yellows and reds.

Gladys stared down to the city life below. All of them huddled and bundled. Couples laughing, sharing a kiss. Kids snug in their fresh winter coats, all dressed up by loved ones and innocently warm. She felt sick to her stomach, and alone. The snuggly lovers and safe little kids always unnerved her. Her hand began to shake with anxiety, and she accidentally dropped the tin can she was clutching.

The unlabeled can fell, rattling on the broken, worn tiles beneath her freezing feet. Gladys bent down creakingly and retrieved the smelly container. The stink made her salivate, and she took her bony old finger and dug inside – scraping up the miniscule globs of Alpo, hungrily savoring the last morsels as she smacked her toothless gums. She returned her gaze outside.

Whatever it was she sensed, be it Death or otherwise, it wasn't a bearer of good tidings. It was closing in with the weather itself. It was very near to her, and ravenous.

If Gladys could only hold it at bay...

Longer, just a little longer.

The power suddenly buckled and snapped out. The bare light bulb above her went black, casting darkness all about her. She moaned and stepped away from the window.

Surveying the gloomy apartment, Gladys gasped in disbelief at just how late it had become. She moved from out of the darkened kitchen and peered into the living room. Shadows already, already everywhere. It was nearly dusk, and the light from the small lamp in the living room was noticeably absent.

"Shit. Shit!"

Gladys was unexpectedly left with no light, no telephone. No nothing. She couldn't panic... did she still even have candles? It seemed they had probably disappeared with everything else she'd lost over the years. There may be one or two. She returned to the kitchen and began rummaging through a drawer of corroded utensils until she found some candles and matches. She crept into the living room and sat down on the ratty couch. The cushion springs dug into her bony skin as she sat waiting until the very last minute to light the wicks. She had to conserve. Gladys watched as the darkness crawled along the floor like a predator, closing in for the kill.

It was coming for her. She could feel it in her very marrow this evening. It seemed to her that so very little time remained. With her power out, and no working telephone - she would be left alone to defend herself. But who would help her? Who in this tenement would help a pathetic old woman? She didn't know anyone, anymore. Gladys hadn't set foot outside the front door in many a year. Many a year. Her groceries and mail brought to her door - the last time she had ventured out, the changes were so great that it seemed like a different world entirely. And now, even more time had passed; time, running out...

The shadows were advancing, gathering forces as they widened and stretched. She didn't have long – soon she would be enveloped in the lurking darkness.

Little ticks and scratches, scrapes and creaks. Gladys could hear them coming, in there - in the dark. She could *sense* them, gaining formation. Soon they would be here, and then they would be upon her. Once that happened, she would certainly be torn to shreds, and nothing would remain of her but dusty bones and withered dry hair.

How could she possibly defend herself? She barely weighed a hundred anymore, wilted and fragile. Gladys' whole body had betrayed her, there was nothing of her left - simply skin and bone. The dog food had left her thin and fragile, but it was all that she had to eat most times.

She barely made rent each month, and that wasn't so costly-considering that this was a slum - but she was bare again after payment. Food. *Food* she was strapped for. Her whole body was constantly wracked with hunger. The empty cans of dog food left open on the counter, now scraped to the nub. She was completely out.

The grocery delivery would be due tomorrow, but the wait seemed like forever. Each Thursday, mysteriously, a scented pink envelope would always arrive, containing fifteen extra dollars. An anonymous gift from one of her old fans, she supposed. She always arranged for fifteen in groceries to be delivered later that same afternoon.

One more day. She could get her groceries in just one more day. Some peanut butter, some bread. Some milk and grits, and a few of pieces of soft fruit. Maybe...maybe if she tipped the delivery boy, he would slip her a couple of extra cans of Alpo, like he had been lately. If she was *extra nice*. She hated to think of it, with that sinister feeling in the air, but she had to plan for days in advance so she wouldn't go hungry. The dog food kept her for two additional days before the next scented letter arrived.

The shadows were getting too close, and Gladys rose and moved back to the kitchen window, where there was some light. She looked out to the bright lamps running throughout the park, glistening off the trees and paths.

The electricity was fine across the street..?

Gladys peered over to the street, and then up along the apartment courtyard. No, *all* the lights were on - the whole building had power...everyone except for her..!

She would need to notify the landlord, immediately. She couldn't remain in a dark apartment overnight, not with the weather all cold and foreboding. Not with...not with...

Gladys dreaded having to use someone else's phone...that meant she would have to go outside of her apartment for the first time in ages. She never, ever found need to venture out into this strange, decaying world...harm was everywhere, closing in.

Harm was *here*, in this very apartment.

There was a light, raspy snigger at the end of the room. Gladys straightened upright, and swung around. She peered deep into the shadows. They stirred oh, so slightly - just a flicker of movement...here or there...

It was *them*.

There was no question.

It had been a while, but she remembered most clearly. She had remembered every day, for decades on end. Oh, yes - it was them, she could tell. These were no mere tricks of the eye, these were *alive*. Quite alive. And dangerous.

She let out a whimper. Why wasn't her power on!?! She had paid all the bills. She always paid the bills. She had failed to pay a few years ago, and a similar storm had come, leaving her freezing for three days before her power returned. She *always* paid bills.

Gladys now had even fewer blankets than she had had back then. Tattered as they were, she would need them to bundle up with if she wanted to survive the cold. Her best plan was to stay out of the shadows, and keep covered on the couch. Gladys gathered what courage she had, and made her way over to the bedroom. She entered the dark room, and crept toward her greasy bed.

The thin burlap and gnarled old quilts had been worn to mere shreds. Some of them weathered down into unusable frays of grimy fabric-the condition of them was miserable. Frayed and smelly and blotchy, they lay in a murky heap on her mattress. Gladys moved over to them, and felt pangs of deep regret. She was suddenly very angry with herself for not stockpiling more before she had become a total recluse.

She gathered up the old quilts and blanket remains, her mind a million miles away, far in the past. Her glory days had seen many a lush bed, many an elegant blanket. Parties and people long gone, long dead. Old, departed, generous days of prosperous youth. They were at the top of the mountain, then. They had feasted on everything - the whole world was theirs for the taking...all their lives before them...

Gladys could see the faces of her splendid lovers, rising up to greet her. They had all been so young, so celebrated. She clutched the bundle of frayed blankets, lost in her past. What had happened to the wealth of beds and lovers? Her gold-plated canopy frames and luxuriant quilts and pillows? Now all she had were these. These seedy old rags of burlap and torn strands. She squeezed the shabby remains, shaking them tightly in her anger.

There was a rattling little titter, and a black talon popped swiftly from the folds of the blankets, snagging deeply into Gladys' left hand. Gladys gasped in shock-the claw was digging in cruelly, like a hook. She could feel the talon scraping against her bones..!

She instinctively dropped the blankets - backing up as the thing clasped onto her wrist with its other hand. The blankets fell away, revealing the lithe creature.

Its black claw dug deeper into her flesh as it leveraged itself onto her arm. Gladys thrashed her arm as the beast clamored up and stabilized a full-body grip. The creature laughed menacingly, its long fingers wrapped securely around her arm. It was clinging to her like a leech. The long, pointed ears unfolded from its slick skull, and it raised its obsidian head to look at her.

Gladys screamed. Bright yellow eyes, with catlike black pupils, calculating and conniving, glared up at her. Ancient, smart as the Devil himself - it grinned wickedly with a long mouth of enormous fangs. "Gladdyyysss!"

Wailing, Gladys slammed the beast against the wall. And again. She beat the black creature against the wall, against the door. She slammed the thing until she could feel it surrender and slide away - the long talons gliding out of her skin like butter. The monster let loose of her and fell onto the discarded pile of blankets, all teeth and eyes and pointed ears. Black. Black as the darkest dread, the most unnatural black. It gnashed evilly at her, its forked tongue gliding over its ferocious teeth in hungry anticipation. The slimy black creature raised a long finger and pointed straight at her, accusingly. There was a sudden burst of sulfur and smoke, and it was gone.

Gladys forgot the blankets, and exited the bedroom. The demon would be back, and there would be others, too. She knew that she was already surrounded. With the shadows they manifested...with the coming of the night. What was she to do?

She shakily went to the kitchen and ran her bleeding hand under the faucet. The water came out all rusted and brown. There was blood everywhere. She took a small, tattered dishtowel off the counter and wrapped it feebly around her shaking hand. Gladys rummaged through her drawers, and managed to find a small paring knife, which she clutched knowingly. It was dull and rusted, but was still deadly.

Her breathing began to level, her elderly eyes scoped the rancid apartment for any other movement - but there was none. Blood soaked the dishtowel and spilled onto the cracked linoleum. She could feel the blood spattering her cold, bare feet. Sniggers erupted from various darkened corners-they were watching, waiting. If only she could see! If only the power were on.

Where had she left her candles? Gladys felt around on her cabinet counters. They weren't here - she had left them on the couch..! Damn fool! She cursed her stupidity. The living room was encased in total darkness by this point!

Gladys had no other choice.

She had to go outside.

The bustling in the corners assured her that more of the demons had manifested. She was sure there was a handful already, waiting hungrily. Maybe if she had light, just a little - she could hold the shadows at bay...maybe hold them off, if even just a little. She had to get to a phone. Had to call the landlord. But only. If only.

The wind beat chill upon the door, the growing moan. It waited out there for her, just as the shadows waited inside - becoming more dangerous with each passing minute. She had to get her power back on - her life depended on it.

Gladys put her decrepit excuse for a coat on, and shoeless - managed to pry open the front door, and step out.

She was snapped by raw cold, the wind thundering around her- thrashing sleet against her skin. Her poor feet already damp and bitten. Gladys looked around at the graffiti littered walls. There was decay everywhere. Everything had turned to shit - it was worse than the last time, years ago.

Gladys swallowed hard, and crept warily down the stairs. She halted at the rail and looked out at the property. The courtyard was strewn with blowing trash and leaves. All the garbage collected at the front of the building. The sleet had slickened everything, all the cars and the driveway. The trees across the way beamed magically in the glow from the street lamps. The frozen ice blew like art through the haze of the arc light.

She crept down the wet concrete stairs to one of the two doors beneath her. Her feet were freezing. She stepped off of the stairway and made her way to the first door ahead of her. The storm whipped her from behind as she bravely went up and rapped urgently at the door. Gladys didn't want to be out here anymore than humanly possible. The quicker she got help, the better.

A young man in a wife-beater came answering, his massive frame filling the doorway. He furrowed his brow as he observed little Gladys, shaking half naked in the cold. Her blood-soaked nightie blowing wildly in the stormy wind.

"Lady...you alright?" he asked.

Gladys stood shaking. "N-N-No. I n-n-need help. My power's turned off, and there's...rats. Trying to attack me. I n-need help. Can I come in and telephone our landlord, and see if he can help me? It's freezing up there."

The man stood stoically in the door frame. He looked off into the apartment, then looked sternly at Gladys. "Lady. I, uh. I don't know if I can do that. You see..."

Gladys held up her wounded hand, dressed in a blood-soaked dish rag. "I'm wounded."

"I can see that, and I'd like to help, but..."

Gladys interrupted, touching his chest. "I'll suck your dick."

The man drew back. "*What* did you say?"

"I'll eat your cum, too. I'll rub it all over. I got no teef-it's hot. You'll cum. Please. Please get me help. I'll..."

Just then the man's pissed off wife came to the door. She pushed the befuddled husband back and took charge. She held a large bowl and whisked mashed potatoes angrily. "I did not just hear what I think I heard. What did you just tell my husband?!"

"Please-I need help..! My power is out and it's absolutely freezing up there and I have no blankets." Gladys held up her punctured hand. "Please, I'm wounded."

The woman stared at her coldly.

"Please. Could I just use the telephone. Could I just call our landlord..?"

"What makes you think I should help you?"

Gladys clasped her frozen hands together, pleading.

"Please."

The woman glared at her piercingly. She had no pity. "Didn't I just hear you say that you would suck my husband's dick? Who the hell do you think you are?!"

Gladys blubbered. "Please-anything. I'm in apartment 14. I'll lick your clit...anything you like. Let me call the landlord..! I need the power back on or I'll die!"

"Listen," the woman said after a brief assessment, "I know about you. I've heard. I want you to turn around and go back to where you came from. I will call the landlord. You just get the hell out of here, and don't come back. You just turn away...and go home."

"Unit 14. I'm in danger. Tell him it's *urgent*..."

"I got it. Just turn around and go home. Right now."

Gladys nodded, then nodded to the man, with a wink. The woman slammed the door shut, and Gladys began her icy ascent up the stairs. The storm lashed at her. She fumbled with her keys as she reached the door, but found it ajar - waiting. She wasn't surprised.

She crawled back into her apartment, which was dry - but just as cold as the outside had been. Gladys leaned back against the door and scanned the depths of her darkened living room. The sopped old coat dripped at her feet, pooling around her. If she truly wanted to survive, she would have to make a dash to the couch area, where she could retrieve her candles and matches. She was sure she had left them on the cushion, she was sure. The creatures couldn't come where there was light, she knew; she remembered. If she could just get her candles lit, she could hopefully ward them off until the power returned...

She could hear them bustling. Skirmishing around within the black. Did she even have time to let her eyes adjust? They were formulating, in there. In the dark.

Gladys knew that the candlelight would be her only protection. That and the knife. The knife? Where was the knife? She dug desperately at the pockets of the dripping wet coat, and found only holes. Had she put it on the counter..? Damn her memory! The candles - the candles were definitely on the couch. She was sure of it.

God, how had it come to this? The sniggering mass that was taunting her confounded her, suddenly. How? *How* had it come to this?

Gladys smacked her gums. Oh, but it had been *good*. Had been *so very good*. How was she to resist? The marvelous temptations and infamy had been handed to her, placed in her lap - and she took it. She ran with it...she excelled in it, all of it. She had been the blow job queen of America..! Gladys salivated, remembering her diva days, remembering all the cock - *all the sweet doggy cock*.

Gladys Gladass - dog porn priestess extraordinaire. Her glory days, long gone - but once...once she had been a *star*. Now all she had were memories. No memorabilia. It had been years since she had pawned her Triple X movie posters, from the pre-beastie days - when all she had done were simple BJs and missionary. Posters from when she was mainstream, before she had met...him. And he changed *everything*.

At first he moved her on to more hardcore features - anal lead into three-ways, three-ways lead into orgies - but as she became intimate with the bearded one - the goateed one, the more she was drawn into his encompassing spell. He had magic, real magic - and offered her infamy and sexual delights beyond compare-blood soaked, and Satanic. Orgies were followed by years of gang-bangs - Gladys could eat cum better than anyone. Loads of men would blast in her face, and even more men paid to see her take it. She was a star.

But then the *forbidden*, the veiny red knot - swollen fat and dripping, ready. Her initial reluctance was quickly subdued as her feelings went from revulsion to compulsion. Bestiality soon grew to be her forte, and Gladys Gladass' reputation as the starlet who would do everything became an actual fact. Any animal, anytime. The bald one treated her to every luxury, every indulgence. He rented her out to all of the best, all the richest. She was a phenomena.

Gladys had become the number one request for the bearded one's demonic acid parties - as she would gang-bang and take animals at the same time, she would take anything. Huge Satanic orgies. Naked, writhing rituals - all the sweat, all the bodies, all the animals and all the cum. And then the blood. And then all the blood...

All the spilt blood.

She remembered.

Ritualistic orgies swathed in blood.

Sacrificial blood.

Her blood.

Her own children's blood...

A daughter, a son.

Now gone.

The bald one, the bearded one, long ago. They all stood chanting -high on acid and loving belief that *this* bald man could possibly summon *Him*, the horned one, the golden ram. Her own children, tied. Placed in the center of the pentangle...she took the knife and cut her own daughter's wrist, cut her own son's wrist. Gladys couldn't hear their pleas as she milked their flowing arms into a golden chalice - all Gladys could hear was the chanting -the conjuring of *He*.

The excited gathering passed the goblet, sharing the children between them. Every ritual had been performed perfectly - surely with the sacrifice of the priestess Gladys' own infants, *He* would find them worthy, and appear. The chanting increased, the mass reaching near-hysteria.

Wind suddenly blew through the cramped room, smelling of roses. All of the coven leaned forward expectantly - would Satan indeed appear? Blood soaked, naked - they twisted anxiously, and chanted. The bearded one took Gladys' hand, the dagger, and lifted it high - guiding her. Gladys seized the spike and pierced her daughter's heart without hesitation.

The gasp from her daughter was so small and vulnerable - it was barely audible, only Gladys could hear. It unexpectedly sunk into her, into her very fiber - later haunting her every sleepless, hungry night.

The candles fluttered out, and the black ones manifested - rupturing forth from the darkness itself. A multitude of the blackened demons fell upon Gladys' screaming little boy and her dead little girl - tearing their ripe little bodies to shreds. Blood splattered the congregation as claws began to fly.

Once the children were devoured, the black monsters turned on the flock without hesitation. The congregation fled away from the scene, suddenly frightened. What were *these*? Where was the Devil..?!. The crowd exploded, the demons jumping them, and cutting them to pieces.

Saying the Lord's Prayer, one of the parish brandished a candle, and the light held the demons at bay. The beasts avoided the light, dodging toward the worshipers in the shadowy areas. The mass huddled together. Gladys stood transfixed by the candlelight. In the arc of the candle's glow, she could discern the black creatures, ancient and eternal - they *blanketed* the altar. All Gladys could see was unmitigated evil, smiling at her. Ready to devour.

These monsters were real, and she was going to die at their discretion. She had spilt her children's blood, only to invite her own death. Suddenly, her mind cleared, and she stood confronted with her own pornography, her own actions. The dog-porn priestess suddenly seemed a fantasy, and repulsive. She could feel the hollowness inside her inner chasm; feel the damnable loss of her very own *soul*.

People lay screaming in pools of their own flesh. Arms and heads were swiftly torn from their sockets. The parish flooded the doorways, and they were all trapped in their bloody doom. Gladys, transfixed, watched the man with the candle, standing untouched by the horde. Had he had enough faith remaining, amidst all his previous Satanic devotions, to propel such a force from the flame? Was there redemption, here - in this very room, before this shadowy, evil onslaught?

Gladys moved with childlike wonder to the glow of the light. If there is time for her fellow sinner, is there then time enough for her own redemption? Gladys reached out to the man as he prayed-she could feel the goodness, feel the Holiness of the light. He reached out his hand to her, offering her salvation - but Gladys was rushed swiftly away by the bearded man, the bald one. Her arm was crushed in his grip, she turned back as the massacre continued - the man with the candle unscathed, protected and Saved, watching her sadly as she was quickly whisked away. The bearded man dashed her off into their limousine, and they escaped naked and bloody, but unharmed.

They were given thick fur coats to cover themselves. Gladys collapsed on the dark leader's shoulder, and she let him pet her hair. "You cannot go to the light, because you are for *Him*," he said, petting. "Nothing will save you. Murderess. You belong to Lucifer, now. You are *His*."

Gladys shook in fear. It was true. The bald one had made her an international star, then compelled her to murder her own children..! She had given everything to him - everything...this man who would abandon her completely.

He soon left Gladys with nothing, just her fading looks. Amazing what age can do to a pornography career. Suddenly she was too old and ugly, and was never in demand. Ruined, Gladys Gladass fell swiftly into bleak obscurity.

Now she was here, freezing, starving and toothless - cornered by shadow - demons in this powerless apartment...

She came back to the present in a sick, vapid awareness. An awareness of loss. Gladys could still recall the inner warmth of the lone candlelight as it shone through the chaos, but trembled with vacant regret. She could never be saved, not at this point, and the punctuation of the enormity of this chasm knocked a punch that bore straight through her. Her time for redemption had come and gone like her wicked, sticky glory days.

Now she was damned.

And she was about to die, and was going to suffer all eternity at the mercy of these black shadow creatures. The same evil demons that had torn apart her coven, the same that were right beside her now. Gladys knew they were with her - just watching, waiting.

She had to survive. Certainly she could find some redemption, some forgiveness - if she could only survive the night..! Gladys knew she could save her filthy soul. If she could just live long enough to find Holy sanction at some church in the morning...if she could manage to snag the matches and candles from the couch across the room, then she could be Saved. She could live, once the flame was lit. The demons were banished in the light. She had seen it before, it would work..!

Gladys made a bolt for it. She barreled into the living room, her arms held in front of her lowered head. She raced to the couch as fast as she could, her wet coat draping over her vulnerable flesh.

She felt the creatures leap on her immediately, scampering up the coat. They hustled around her legs, swiping at her. Sharp fangs burrowed into her right arm as a ram-horned demon flew onto her. Blood soaked the black little face. She was almost to the couch. Another demon clambered up her left leg, digging deep into her flesh with its claws. The sharp nails gouged her and tore her open.

Gladys reached the couch as an extremely large demon pounced onto her back. The monster dug deeply into her ribs and bit cruelly into her left shoulder. The weight of the creature brought her down, and she smacked her head on the edge of the couch. Gladys pulled herself up to the cushions, feeling about. The beasts bit into her, enveloped her. She felt along the weathered cushions.

They weren't there. The candles weren't there..!

"Oh, no."

The creatures lashed at her, spitting at her. She tried to cover herself, but the monsters hustled together and flipped her over, onto her back. Several smaller ones had mounted her - rough black penises rubbing against her. The creatures pulled her arms away, and then smaller ones scrambled up to her face and began clawing her with their small, refined talons.

Gladys kicked as hard as she could, her bloody nightie riding up, revealing her worn old crotch. The demons scampered upon her, mounting -digging into her. The small, quick ones jabbed at her face strategically. One demon slipped a swift onyx talon directly under her left eyelid, tearing it slowly off. Skin ripped from her skull. Gladys wailed as the hot blood shot into her exposed eyeball.

Another, dog-sized demon stuck her hand in its treacherous maw and tore three of her fingers off. The tendons pulled, spurting, then snapped away. Gladys' annihilated hand shot streams of blood. Gladys convulsed with the pain. The demons had her spread-eagle, and began lifting her abrasioned husk off the floor.

They began carrying her, dying and bleeding - off toward the bedroom. She sobbed, and could see - with her one good eye, a bright, fiery light manifesting from the kitchen nook. She cocked her head and watched in horror at the sentient monster formulating within her kitchen roost.

The shadow-demons drug Gladys' shredded body up onto the seedy mattress. She couldn't take her gaze off of the enormous figure in the kitchen. Bathed in the fiery light, it began to move, turning towards her.

The bright orange eyes glared cruelly, the massive, horned head of a goat. The long, forked tongue wrapped hungrily around its piercing fangs.

The small, black demons tore open the remains of her nightie, revealing her aged and withered old body, now decimated. Blood spurted from her torn eyeball, and the other eye - wide, and horrified - stared fearfully to the horned behemoth.

The creatures bowed as the enormous fiend approached. "Master."

"His Majesty."

Even backlit in the mysterious orange light she can see *it*. In the doorway, coming to her-the silhouette of Lord Satan's gargantuan, three-prong penis. It swung mightily as it neared her. Erect and starving - needing release more than anything. Bursting. The largest cock was red, fat and thick, and five feet long.

Gladys was spread open missionary, and the biggest prong was going in first, she knew, and would rip her to pieces. The other two would scrape her bottom remains.

She struggled to break free, but the black demons held her fast. There was no escaping for old Gladys now - it was her very end.

The colossal penis found her wilted lips and pressed.

It was dreadful, as big as her whole body.

Gladys didn't know how she would manage to take it - but she knew. She knew. She knew she would take it all.

STUDIES IN SCARLET
An Anthology of Mystery

Volume One

CRIME SCENE DO NOT CROSS

Available on www.lulu.com

FLOWER IN THE WIND

By

Rick McQuiston

Paula watched as tiny pebbles and dirt cascaded down from high above, creating an empty symphony in the cave. The echoes reverberated throughout the space and although she had grown mildly accustomed to them they still affected her in many ways. They tapped into her mind trying to fracture the delicate barrier between sanity and insanity.

Occasionally a stray memory wandered into her conscience and struggled for validity but fought against the erosion of time, which substantially diluted each and every one regardless of their sentimentality or importance.

The memory that most steadfastly attempted to be recognized and appreciated was of her fiancé Tom. She could still see his wavy blonde hair and crystal blue eyes. She could still smell his masculine and attractive aroma. She could still hear his soft but confident voice say I love you. All of these things still remained in her mind and were her only connection to her comfortable and loving past, a past that was slipping away like a flower in the wind.

The wind. She shuddered at the thought of it. It was the cause of the catastrophic situation she, and very likely the rest of the world, was in. High, relentless, gusty winds; and not just normal gales but mind numbing, destructive and all encompassing ones, enveloping all before them in a non-discriminatory embrace of devastation.

She walked towards the opening of the cave and carefully pulled out a small oval shaped stone from the hastily constructed wall that she and the others had assembled. Instantly, the ear splitting howls of the wind permeated the cave. Peering out displayed only what she already knew, a vast and featureless terrain.

"Smooth as glass," the voice behind her said. It was Roy. His six-foot frame towered over her petite form and he outweighed her by at least fifty pounds. "Nothing left out there but flat land…and the wind of course."

She whirled around to face him. His pockmarked face, from a severe bout with chicken pox when he was a young boy, glared down at her. A wry smile slid across his features like water in a bucket of oil.

"Roy, do you mind?" she said sternly. She knew that he coveted her love and had even gotten into a drunken brawl with Tom once over her. She also knew that she must be careful. Tom was not around to protect her anymore.

Roy stood in her way. He used his size to intimidate others, which was one of the many traits that she detested in him. She had wished many times that he would have been swept away by the wind instead of Tom but unfortunately that was not the case.

"Becky needs me. I have to change the dressing on her wounds." She brushed past him as quickly as she could, careful not to anger him. That would only complicate the dire situation they were already in.

There was only him, his teenage cousin Becky and Louise, a neighbor girl who happened to be riding her bike by Paula's house when the worst gales started to hit. She had managed to escape with them just in time.

"Paula," Becky moaned in a weak voice. "Will you come here please? I'm very thirsty."

The dark corner where she lay was full of rocks and crawled with bugs. Paula felt bad for her and wished there was a more comfortable spot for her. She scurried over to Becky and began to collect the small, dirty plastic cups they had scattered around the cave to gather water. What little water trickled down from the ceiling barely was enough to sustain one person much less four. She gave the cups to Becky who greedily sucked them down.

"Why bother with her?" Roy growled. "You know as well as I do she's not gonna make it."

"She's your cousin!" Paula shouted back.

Roy gritted his teeth and scowled, "I don't give a crap if she's Marilyn Monroe, we shouldn't be wasting water on her! She's not gonna make it!"

Paula reared back and slapped him. She immediately regretted it, not because he didn't deserve it, but because she realized that they could not afford to fight amongst themselves. They needed to work together if they were going to survive.

Roy stared at her. The red mark across his face glared brightly and contrasted strongly with his pale skin. But to her surprise and relief he simply walked away. Becky looked up at Paula, tears streaming down her battered face.

"He's right you know," she whispered. "You shouldn't waste time on me."

Paula bent down and gave her a hug. "Don't worry. We'll get through this."

****

The broken anemometer sat near the cave's entrance. She had managed to grab it at the last minute and threw it in her bag. Why she did she didn't know other than it might be the only part of her little brother Joey that she would have left. He had been an amateur meteorologist of sorts and had several devices used for measuring and observing weather conditions. She fondly recalled him spewing out various information about topics regarding weather. He had bought the anemometer through a catalog and had altered it to be very accurate with his own parts. He added gauges and fittings and cups to the existing ones and painted it a bright red. It was one of his most cherished pieces of equipment.

The dial he added gave a clear and fairly accurate reading of wind speed. She had fastened it to the ground just outside the cave when they had first arrived and had pulled it back in before it blew away. She looked at the gauge. The glass was cracked badly but the reading was still legible...one-hundred and two miles per hour, and that was a few days ago, the gusts had increased rapidly and steadily since then. She guessed they were probably near one hundred and fifty miles per hour, perhaps more.

"Kinda tempting isn't it?" Roy's voice seemed to emanate from the darkness itself. "Just to walk out into the wind and let it take you. Ya get to see the world." His face appeared in the blackness followed by the remainder of his body. "It'll be like flying, soaring as high as you could wanna go."

Paula steadied her nerves as best she could. "You're tired Roy," she reasoned. "You need some rest. I'll get you a blanket." She reached for her bag and withdrew a tattered quilt that her mother had sewn when she was a little girl. Roy rushed forward and seized her wrist.

"We could go together. Imagine it, the two of us flying high, seeing the world," he said.

She yanked her arm from his grasp. "You need some sleep," she retorted angrily and walked back to her spot in the cave. She could feel his eyes watching her and knew very well that he was beginning to lose his mind.

Sleep did its best to elude her but sheer exhaustion, both physically and mentally, eventually won out as she fell into a deep and troubled slumber. She dreamt of Tom pulling his truck into her driveway to pick her up for a date. She dreamt of her father working on his hot rod in the garage. She dreamt of her mother cooking up her famous tuna casserole. She dreamt of her brother Joey excitingly running around the house when his latest piece of equipment came in the mail. She even dreamt of Fred, her bloodhound, wiling away the days on the front porch. She dreamt of all these things from her past which were unmistakably tainted with the painful stain of reality.

Her sleep was broken by the sound of stones crumbling. She jerked awake and flung her gaze towards the entranceway of the cave.

Roy was there, standing directly in front of the wall and carefully, almost delicately, removing stones from it. He already had several smaller rocks tossed aside and was working on dislodging a large one from the center as the howls of the wind were beginning to permeate the cave causing the ceiling to rain down dirt and pebbles.

Paula leapt to her feet and ran to him screaming for him to stop. "Roy what are you doing?" she cried. "You'll kill us all!" she could hear the gusts of wind grow stronger as they tried to enter through any opening they could.

Roy easily pushed her to the ground and increased his effort in removing the large stone. "I'm gonna see the world," he laughed. "Top of the world, ma, I'm gonna be on top of the world!"

Paula grabbed a grapefruit sized rock and flung it with all her might at Roy. Her aim proved good and it landed squarely on the back of his head. He collapsed to the ground cursing at her. Paula realizing the opportunity scuttled over to where he lay and frantically began pulling her shoelaces out to tie him up with. But the wall had been compromised by Roy's efforts and started to crumble right before her eyes.

"You dumb broad," Roy hissed through bloody teeth. "I want to fly, do you hear me? I want to fly!"

He reached up and grabbed Paula's ankle and flipped her onto her back. The blood was literally pouring from his wound coating both of them in a sticky mess of crimson.

"I'll teach you to stop me," he growled. He stood up and digging his hands into the wall yanked a large stone near the center out. The wind immediately whipped in through the opening and flung everything, including Paula, Louise and Becky against the back wall of the cave. Roy hung on and began to crawl through the hole.

The sight of his skin being peeled back like a ripe piece of fruit was too much for Paula to bear; she buried her and the girl's faces in the blanket. She made the mistake however, of looking up one last time just when Roy reached the outside of the cave and was sucked away with such force that he did not even have time to make a sound.

She forced her way back to the wall. Her face and hands stung terribly from the wind and she could feel the blood begin to cover her, but she managed to reach the wall and push the rock back into place. Thirty exhaustive minutes later she had the only barrier between them and death reasonably rebuilt and secure.

Behind her she could hear Becky and Louise crying. As if the situation they were in were not bad enough, they also had the loss of loved ones haunting their feelings. But at least Roy was gone, of that much they could be grateful for.

Paula walked over to the girls. She wasn't their mother or even a friend but she knew she had to be the one to be strong if they were going to survive. Cradling their heads in her arms she joined them in sobbing.

****

Hours passed with no lessoning of the wind. It continued to relentlessly swirl and gust in a song of nature promising death. It had flattened everything in sight to a smooth, featureless plain, void of civilization. The incredible power it displayed was beyond anyone's comprehension or understanding. It was controlling the Earth, tossing aside puny humans at its whim.

Paula sat up and wondered if there was anything left of the outside world. She knew there must be an explanation for the wind. There was little doubt in her mind that there were many scientists and researchers who could easily explain it but that was of little comfort to her or the girls, or any of the people who had been wiped out. Would they be able to stop it? She doubted it. How could someone stop high winds, especially ones that reached hundreds of miles per hour? Nothing built by man could withstand such a pounding onslaught.

She looked over at Becky and Louise; they were fast asleep next to one another behind her. Their faces masked the pain and fear that she knew lurked below the surface. They were both so young, much younger than she was, and like her they still had so much to live for.

And then she heard it. It was faint almost to the point of being non-existent but it was definitely there; a low, soft voice...Tom's voice, and it was calling her name...from outside the wall.

"Pauuullaa. Paulaaa, it's me Tom."

The wind diluted the clarity of the words greatly but she was still able to decipher them somewhat.

"Are you in there Paula? Pauullaaa..."

Torn between the joy of hearing his voice and common sense she felt herself crawl towards the entrance way of the cave. Becky and Louise were still sound asleep and oblivious to the impending danger they faced otherwise they surely would have tried to stop her.

She reached the wall and began to remove a small stone near the top. Logic and the instinct to survive were pushed aside by her longing to see her beloved fiancé again, to hold him in her arms and to kiss his lips once more. Dehydration constricted her throat making it nearly impossible to utter a response to the voice other than a low groaning.

"Paauullaaa. Paauullaaa.."

Any hint of malevolence in the words was masked by the source of them. Her financé, the man who she was going to escape with to the big city and pursue her dream of having a family. The man she was going to spend the rest of her life with as Mrs. Thomas Kannery. The man she was going to grow old with.

"Paaulla…I'm here. It's me Tom."

Against her better judgment she pulled the small stone out.

Hesitation gripped her mind, momentarily causing her to pause in looking out of the opening. She was scared. However, she was also surprised at how well she had dealt with the situation so far and had faith in herself that she never had before.

She had also developed a special bond with the two girls and felt a responsibility for them.

And then she looked out of the hole.

The wind hissed in her face with a ferocity that was terrible to behold. It was still an unyielding behemoth of nature unmatched by all before it. Shielding her eyes as best she could, she strained to see the outside world.

At first, nothing was visible, only the roiling, empty void of nothingness that had cursed her eyes and mind so many times before.

But then, an image appeared. A vague silhouette of a face materialized approximately five feet from the wall. Gradually a body formed beneath the face and melted into it giving it a full image of a person.

It was Tom, her beloved fiancé who had been taken by the wind! He looked at her and smiled. It was a loving and familiar smile.

"Hello, Paula," he said through the assault from the wind, which was whipping his blonde hair all about his face.

She was speechless; words failed her completely. The impossibility of what she was seeing was matched only by her desire for it to be real.

"Tom, is it really you?" she stammered like a schoolgirl.

A look of frustration washed over his face. "Do you doubt your own eyes?" he asked.

"Should I? I want for it, for you, to be real but I'm not a child. I know it can't be." What she was saying hurt her almost as much as the wind slapping her face.

He turned away from her, lifted his arm and gestured to a desolate spot behind him in the distance. Paula strained to see what he was pointing at. She saw a small object jutting out of the ground but could not discern exactly what it was. Tom raised both arms and approached the wall. Bringing his hands closer together he formed a barrier that shielded the wind from the opening in the wall.

"You must look closely now," he instructed. "You must see through the winds."

She leaned forward and marveling at how he had managed to obstruct the winds with just his hands, focused on the object and at last she was able to see what it was. It was a flower, a single, bright red flower that resembled a rose.

How could it survive in the wind? She concluded that it could by the same means by which she was talking to her dead fiancé.

"It's a sign...of survival. It shows that there is always hope, that anything can survive if it has faith."

Paula felt an enormous weight lifted from her shoulders. For the first time since the nightmare began she felt hopeful. Tom smiled as he lowered his arms, forcing her to shield her face from the winds again and back away from the hole even though she did not want to.

"I must go now," he lamented. "But I have something for you." He lifted his arm and produced a small red flower similar to the one in the distance behind him. "To remember me by...forever."

Paula reached out and quickly snatched it from him. Her hand bled from the biting wind, but she paid it little notice. All that mattered was the flower and what it represented.

His smile embedded itself in her heart long after he had faded away into nothingness. The empty space where he had stood hurt far worse than the wind, which seemed to be increasing yet again. She reluctantly forced the stone back into its spot on the wall and using what little water they had, mudded it back into place.

Outside the wall, the flower began to swell. Its pedals wilted and turned a sickly, dirty white in color as enormous, pulsating spores jettisoned out from its center to be carried by its wind to all corners of the globe for germination. All around it writhing tentacles sprouted up and flailed in the gales like insane dancers as translucent slime coated its entire mass. It was aware and intelligent and gyrated from side to side in a grotesque mockery of laughter. An image of Thomas Kannery formed at its base and smiled. It had been easy... *real easy.*

Paula sat back down on her blanket and looked at the girls, they were still sound asleep. Even the chaos of the wind coming into the cave when she removed rock didn't stir them to consciousness; sheer exhaustion controlled their bodies beyond any doubt. She lifted the flower and inhaled its fragrance. The aroma was strange, almost unrecognizable, but she realized that it had been awhile since she had last smelled a flower. She set it on the ground beside her blanket and laid down. Sleep visited her quickly and transported her to its peaceful realm; a welcome and much needed diversion from reality.

The flower arched itself upright and its pedals started to wilt as they changed to a sickly, dirty white color. And then it began to swell.

DAMNATION OBSERVES

By

Nickolaus A. Pacione

Observers all of us are, or were, in our time and the madness that wanders from an illness no one can see or understand. The things that are prescribed by religion of how a mind works or dwells, the descending or talking down upon an illness they are too scared to know or understand – because the end result from the illness becomes a damnation they say or know all too well. Damnation – the word we heard all too often just because of what, we're sick? And the sickness we have is the kind they can't know or want to understand – the sickness of the mind.

The scars we carry across the wrists because of the blood we've drawn from them with cold steel. What they see or want to know – justify that the madness is that of the demons or unclean angels they wish to believe drives us. Offer salvation from ourselves when we want none, looking to the nonexistent heavens waiting for someone to heal us, but no one is there. Just the silent observer, as we're the vocal observer. Someone who offers us a black leather bound book with gold rimmed pages saying this is the medication for an illness that can't be seen or heard.

"Follow me," one of them said, a younger female. She didn't

have a name but her sincerity stood in the eyes of those who knew this darkness, but yet has no understanding how an illness of the mind ticks away. It is a clock and a nightmare – the invitation was declined for her to have me follow. I said no because there was a horror she couldn't understand or want to. The madness descending as she watched was nothing she could really imagine or fathom – the effects of a nightmare in a living world, the nightmares induced by higher doses of pills that are supposed to better the mind. I looked and made direct eye contact. The nihilism within the eyes of those who dwell in the wide awake nightmare draws the individual who doesn't understand into a world that takes years to understand even their own sickness.

"Damnation observes everything, damnation watches everyone – damnation is the observer of madness," I explained to her. She had no idea what I meant by that, but as she looked further she saw the nightmares as they are or were; a past of madness looking to catch up with someone as they are in the present or future. Madness is as it becomes a hell no one understands or wants to begin to see. The witness of such becomes in the realms of the mentally ill, and as myself, this was a darker place some try to fathom or put an explanation on. Either way as some pastors or greeters tried to paint a mental illness as a demonic experience, it isn't that but something even darker than something they paint in the Holy Book about the Lake of Flames.

Her puzzled look said everything and nothing. She had no idea how the nightmares inside the mind of a sick man illustrates itself. The depths visited are the things she can't return from and the nightmares wandering inside the eternal winters of a madness-laden mind. Dredging within a world of needles in the veins and pills that are supposed to heal the mind – just to take them into a horror deeper within the realms of madness and fatality. Both seem go to hand in hand, like a dysfunctional marriage, yet the dreams within the madness echo limitless ends of fatality. Horrors in hell are insanity – waiting for different results from the same actions. Madness wanders looking in the abyss as a mind wanders within the winters of eternity – damnation observes when it begins, the nervous breakdowns and the medication induce the nightmares as they are taken one step further. The observers holding the black book with gold rimmed pages had no idea how far the darkness they knew would descend – the horrors within the nightmares they don't want to imagine become imagined. Such nightmares begin when damnation observes, and when it comes – something gruesome this way forever comes.

"Follow us," the younger woman said as they stood there with their leather bound book with gold pages in their hands. She wore a long grey dress that reached the ankles and a cloak that covered her head – but all the mind, she wandered among the streets with the leather bound book in hand with gold pages. The younger woman watched and the shadows rose from the dying concrete – wandering as they were if they were alive for a number of centuries. She started to wander among the streets and noticed the smell of death around her – yet everyone around here still was quite alive. Somewhere around watching, she wandered frightened praying to the empties skies for the horror to pass, yet something gruesome this way comes. The madness she sees becomes the witness of all she hears as the entire earth quakes beneath her feet.

"What is happening?" she heard herself saying in the back of her head.

"Nightmares coming to life, and all the madness awakening when damnation observes. I know you don't believe in nightmares coming to life, but in some ways these are your darkest of nightmares as they are slowly awakening," I said with a calm voice.

"Why me and why this place?" she asked as she became more afraid.

"Your faith in God, and how it doesn't agree with the sickness unseen. The things that are not said among the pews. All the sermons you heard preached will never tell you about the true sick from the ones who are physically ill. I've seen this kind of sick and am one of those kinds of sick. The modern leper within the shadows I am – the madness that becomes real when it is disconnected through life with chemistry. Disconnected because the entire society around us is eternally snowed – snowed and hollow-eyed as you are now."

Madness dwelling as we are, madness as we once were. Among the nightmares and reality as they both intertwine within a darkness no one awakes from. The believer watched as this darkness awakened waiting from the keeper of the eyes as they watched. Deeper down as it was seen from a darkness in a world, and that becomes the echo of what it was like without a faith of any kind. The idea frightened her in the truth being --- we're all on our own. No God – no Christ to leave for salvation, and it was in this a dwelling nightmare they can't imagine or fathom. There was none – just as damnations observes.

"What is this world?" she asked in horror shielding herself with the black leather bound book with gold tinged pages. This world was described in the eyes of both Dante and Milton – a world that paradise is forever lost. She couldn't understand why some people have to function with blood and medicine in their veins that the doctors around them help create... a godless dystopia. Godless. One way for the eyes of the mentally ill making it easier to illustrate the darker world around them outside the pews they once called home. Medicine in the veins causing the world around them to turn a pale shade of green; death and sleep become closely related because when sleep happens it takes a duration of days, leading one to a threshold of darkness.

The woman in grey followed within the shadows that descended between the world of the sleeping and the world of the dead. This world she stepped into, the nightmares she wandered in – became the echoes of someone's torment, and the echoes of someone's unseen sickness. In the eyes of Damnation, one either sees a route of madness or the route of salvation, just as it brings one further in the places some can't fathom. She watched and wandered, waiting – looking for a way out of the madness, in a nightmare full of statues who were once living. Cold as stone they were, watching back at her asking for help they would never receive.

"What is this world?" she whispered to herself, descending further down into the hallways of pale green and floors of black. She wandered around in this madness looking for a way out. All she found was a place that everyone sees in their most distorted of nightmares. The sound of her own heart pounding in a frantic pace was the only thing she could hear now, and the horror dwelling within the eternal battle of science and belief waited around her and the surroundings as she stood there.

"Am I in the nightmare of a man who is snowed?" she asked with a frantic tone to her voice. This was one of the places where damnation observes, waiting as a man who was knocked out from science and chemistry. The chemical madness she watched within the walls she walked around in. What she smelled was something cold, and something without a soul. She had no idea that she was dragged into a nightmare from someone who was induced by hypnotics. Hypnotics – medications used in the same reason that people are giving a sedative; to help people who have a history of racing thoughts sleep. Further as she was brought into the abyss of cold stone, and the understanding within a madness watched – as an entity it was, further as she descended, it became the wandering horror after damnation observes. She watched, and with a bewildering landscape surrounding her, the madness within the hall of bright green and soulless black swallowed everything around her. It was an entity of its own making.

"Where am I? Dear God – where am I?" she tried to scream but nothing came out. The lady in Victorian grey watched as all the nightmares she didn't want to imagine came to life, and the mental illness she tried to deny was becoming an entity she didn't want to imagine. She did try to pray, but no answers to her prayers were found within a world without a God. She was a woman of sincere faith walking around in the mind of someone with none. I was a man without a soul, bringing a woman into his depths within the nightmares. Something she couldn't fathom the madness descended into something true. She saw horrors as they wandered as entities in the eyes and mind.

Sick or disturbed as someone wanders within their mind – the realms are yet to be revealed as she was pulled further into the surfaces wandering as a zombie; blind within a cloaking shadows. Aimless as she felt, trying to ask for a light from her God, but received nothing only emptiness and a hallow-eyed silence. Wandering. Watching as an observer of the damned – she waited among the passages that became the depths of some immortal nightmares

"What is going on? Could someone tell me exactly where in God's name I am?" she screamed but nothing came through the lime green walls. Her words descended into the mind of the snowed. She watched, waited and trudged within a darkness. She couldn't hear the salvation that she tried to pray for. Madness she seen and horrors she knew, but all that she tried to deny that couldn't be ignored. She whispered and heard nothing, eyes wandered into the depths. She tried to imagine what was the description of eternal darkness as the world around her.

She stood in complete silence, mouth agape and waiting for the moment to scream but she couldn't even leave a single sound. Just as she was wandering nervously into the depths of the nightmares, and wandered among the mind as she was the observer of the horrific details she wasn't able to handle. Some would end up dead and cold from watching her.

"Welcome to the madness, I am the man who observes as it becomes the entity within a darkening reality," I said to her. "You might pray to God for a long suffering deliverance from a foreboding madness, but no one listens here. On your knees, you pray just for something that will never happen. The horrors become when reality damnation observes."

A faith that couldn't save her, and what dredged in the shadows were the beginning of the madness that some can't imagine. Madness I see, and madness I've known; all too familiar with the horrors left inside. Nightmares as they are within the statues standing in the depths of a human psyche – wandering in a where there are no angels or demons. These are the depths of the mentally disturbed mind that truly did frighten the Christian woman. Her nightmares were shaped in form of the old musty buildings seen in horror films, but yet she doesn't want to imagine things like that exist. The things are pure and lovely for some, while for others they are nightmarish and hauntingly perverse.

Her screams were lost within the abyss known as the dreams of the mentally ill, and those are smeared in an eternal darkness drowned in silence for the rest of ones memory.